DAGGER

S.L. STERLING

Dagger

S.L. STERLING

CHAPTER 1

Dagger

I sᴀᴛ and looked up at the clock that hung on the pale-yellow cement wall. My head was pounding, and a pool of blood was building on the floor in between my feet. The wait times here were getting ridiculous. It was a good thing it wasn't a matter of life or death, I thought to myself. I had been waiting for over two hours before they had finally acknowledged I was even in the waiting room.

It was busy tonight; not as busy as some of the other nights I had been here, but that's what I get for having to come into the emergency room on a Friday night. At least I made it through registration where they had taken my blood pressure and other vitals, and listened to my heart, then the blond behind the desk sent me here, into this hellhole of a waiting room. Across the way a child cried out and I glanced around at the other patients who sat there waiting, just like me, to be seen by the next available doctor.

While I waited, I thought back to the first time I had come walking in here and chuckled to myself. It had been a bad fight that night and I was a fucking mess. At that time, I was still an amateur in the ring and hadn't quite learned the concept of blocking.

The nurses who were on that night had taken one look at me as I walked through the door and had rushed me in to see a doctor. There was no messing around, none of the now usual "go sit in a corner and wait." Both of my eyes were swollen shut, my nose was bloodied and broken, I had a mouth full of blood from a cut on my inner cheek, and a large gash on my head, and I was clutching my side as if I had been shot. I was sure they thought so too, due to the blood-soaked shirt I had been wearing. They had cleaned me up a little, and within minutes, I was on my way down for a CT scan and X-rays to make sure I didn't have any type of brain trauma or broken bones.

Once all the results were in and I had been stitched up and put back together, they had released me. Shortly after that visit I had become a regular and normally came in with the same type of injuries on a monthly basis. Apparently, you become less of an emergency once they find out that you are doing this to yourself, and now they make you wait.

"Hey, Dagger. Another fight I see. Tell me you at least look better than the other guy?" one of the regular night nurses said as she walked by, handing me a clean towel to hold to the cut above my eye. "Make sure you're keep pressure on it. That will help stop the bleeding."

"I know, I know. This isn't the first time this has happened you know," I grumbled, nodding, and held the clean towel she had given me up to my eye. I took the other blood-soaked towel and dropped it into the bin labeled bio-hazard. I sat back against the chair, ignoring the sharp, agonizing pain that shot down my back. There were times lately I felt as if I were being punished for the choices I had made in life. It wasn't my fault I had grown up fighting in the streets. Besides, having a drunk of a father at home, I'd had no choice but to learn how to defend myself at a young age, first from him, and then from the others who picked on me and stole what little lunch money I had. However, if I hadn't learned then, I probably wouldn't be sitting here now. Instead I would have become some nameless victim and my body would have been found facedown in a ditch or back alley somewhere.

Regardless, fighting was now in my blood, so it was no surprise I had made a career out of it. Becoming an MMA fighter was probably the best thing I could have done. I was good at what I did, one of the best in the area, as a matter of fact, and it paid the bills. However, it just so happened that this career choice also came with a lot of injuries. Good thing I was a tough son of a bitch.

"Still kicking ass and takin' numbers, huh, Dagg?" Bree, one of the nurses, said as she entered the room carrying a clipboard. Bree had looked after me the last few times I came in. "Come with me. I had a feeling you might stop in tonight. We haven't seen you in a while. I was getting a little worried," she said as she pulled open a curtain to one of the little exam rooms and patted the paper-covered bed.

I listened to the familiar sound of paper crinkling beneath me as I took a seat and groaned from the pain shooting up my back again.

"I'm just going to take your temperature, blood pressure, pulse, and oxygen saturation, but you probably know the drill by now." She smiled.

"Yep, sure, use and abuse me, just like all the pretty girls." I chuckled and extended my free arm so she could put the cuff on while continuing to hold the towel up to my head. One thing about head wounds: they bleed like a bitch.

I let her do her thing, watching the monitors on the machines. "Why are you here, Dagger? Everything is normal, same as it always is."

"I missed you ladies here at the good ol' emergency room. You guys always take such good care of me, and being a single man, a lady's touch is always nice. Plus, my coach dropped me off here and made me come in." I winked at her as she tore the cuff from my arm and smirked.

She pulled the towel away from my head and checked out my face. Taking her gloved hand, she gently touched the cut above my eyebrow, causing me to jump. She pushed my hand back up, so the towel rested against the cut again, and went to a drawer and pulled out a couple of bandages.

"For the time being, I will butterfly suture this until you see the doctor. It should help stop the bleeding a bit. You'll probably need stitches again."

"Yeah, as you can see, that is the same as always too," I said, looking her in the eyes as she looked over my face again. I flinched this time as she touched another spot under my left eye. I had taken a left hook to that cheek; hadn't even seen it coming until I felt the hit.

"That is probably going to be a lovely shade of green and purple in the coming hours."

She pulled the towel down away from my face and examined the gash closer this time. "Yep, you are going to need stitches. Hold still, this might sting." She smiled at me, while placing the bandages across the gash. I shrugged it off as if I didn't care that I needed to be sewn back up, but, honestly, I hated stitches, and Bree knew it.

Bree was always good to me, and she gently fastened the gash closed with the bandages. "However, this time you should probably come in and have us remove the stitches, instead of doing it yourself." She tsked. "It says here that you left with twelve last time, but you never came back for your follow-up."

"Yeah, yeah. I know, I was short on time," I said, standing up. It was the same lecture as the last time and the time before that. I had become good at removing stitches on my own.

"Every time you remove them on your own, you risk the fact that the wound may not be closed properly and subjecting yourself to infection," she scolded.

"Well, what can I say, I'm a glutton for punishment." I shrugged, smiling.

"Don't flash me that sexy smile of yours. It's serious." She frowned at me and muttered something under her breath as she marked something down on my chart. "All right, you know how it goes now. Take a seat out there." She pulled the curtain open, signaling for me to go and sit down.

"Yep, I know how it goes, go wait and you'll call me as soon as there is a room ready." I grabbed my sweatshirt and walked out into the waiting room. I suddenly realized I spent entirely too much time here. I practically could have done the full check-in myself.

I was just about to head over to where I had been sitting but noticed my seat had now been taken by an older man, and the room was twice as full as it was when I had left. I walked across the room and grabbed a different seat over in the corner, off by myself. This time when I sat down, the pain in my kidney area was bad enough that it ensured me I would probably be peeing nothing but blood in a few hours. Sadly, I knew that feeling too. Guess I probably should have told Bree about the multiple kicks and punches I had endured to that area tonight as well, and perhaps she might have sped things along.

I shrugged off that thought and threw my sweatshirt on, pulling the hood up over my head to cover my eyes. The least Bree could have done was pass me a couple of pain pills on the sly, and she might have if I had told her I had a headache. I felt like shit, and the last thing I wanted was to have a bunch of people sitting and staring at me as if I were some monster out of a movie. Few people in the area new who I was, and I didn't want them to think I was just some looser who had lost in a street fight. I had too much pride to allow them to think that. I would never waste money on a stupid street fight.

The longer I sat there leaning up against the wall using my hood as a pillow the more comfortable I became. Finally, the pain in my back settled and I was just about to fall asleep when I heard another familiar voice call my name.

"Mollie, is that you?" I asked as I pulled the hood off my head and carefully rubbed my half-swollen shut eyes.

"Yeah, Dag, it's me. Come on, handsome, let's get you looked after, shall we?"

I stood up, blinking hard trying to see where I was going. I walked toward the door to the exam rooms, right where Mollie stood. I smiled as I approached her. I had seen her plenty of times here before as well. "Hey, Mollie, are you finally showing your old pal to a room?"

"Yeah, come on, you poor thing," she said, her voice full of pity, grabbing my arm and walking beside me to keep me from banging into things. "Just a warning, I'm not your nurse tonight. You've got the new girl, so make sure you're on your best behavior and that you treat her nicely, okay, Dagger?"

"I'm insulted! When have I ever been mean?" I asked innocently enough to make her laugh.

Even though I couldn't see it, I could imagine her rolling her eyes at me. "When aren't you? You're always impatient, snappish, and the looks you give are enough to knock people to their knees," she said as she pulled the curtain back for me to enter the little cubicle of a room.

"The look you're referring to is part of my charm," I answered, sitting down on the table. "Really, though, the attitude is just because of the pain, Mollie. You guys poke and prod around; it hurts more than the actual fight," I argued, defending my behavior.

She placed my chart in the holder on the wall and went to pull the curtain across. "Well then stop the fighting and be nice, Dagger. The girl looking after you tonight is new here and she isn't used to you yet. She's a sweet girl, so don't give her a hard time. Her and the doctor should be in very soon," she said as she pulled the curtain back across the doorway and left the room.

I sat there for a few moments until the pain got so bad

I had to lay back. I pulled my sweatshirt over my head and kicked my feet up on the gurney, resting my arm across my abs, and closed my eyes. Seconds later, I balled my sweat-shirt up and shoved it under my head to use as a little pillow and laid there staring up at the ceiling. I could barely wait to see what little mouse of a girl they sent in to take care of me. If Mollie had warned me to be on my best behavior, this girl must be weak.

Within minutes, a woman walked into the room wearing cute purple scrubs and carrying a clipboard. She didn't greet me or look at me; she just walked over to the wall and removed my chart, setting it on the counter. I couldn't help but check her out; she had an ass that any man would be foolish to forget. When she looked at me, I felt my pulse start to rise. She had gorgeous glass-blue eyes and long, dark eyelashes, perfect lips, and the cutest nose. Her hair was pulled back in a messy ponytail. She sat down and slipped on a pair of frameless glasses and started going over my chart.

"Could you please remove your T-shirt so I can hook you up to the monitors. If we must shave you, we will," she said, showing me a razor blade.

"No need," I answered as I pulled my shirt over my head. I watched her eyes dance over my chest. I wanted to see if there was any reaction from her, but she just went about her business placing the electrodes on my chest, then she pressed a few buttons and the monitors started to beep. As her fingers grazed over my bare chest, lead to lead, the steady beeping from the machines started to get faster, the numbers climbing.

"Are you feeling okay?" she questioned as she continued to attach the pads and fiddle with the wires. I had been through this a thousand times—it was all just part of the protocol—but this time it was my attraction to her that was causing the machines to go haywire.

"Yeah," I said, swallowing hard.

"Whoa!" she exclaimed as the numbers continued to climb. "Something here has got to be defective." She rested her hand against my chest. "You're sure you feel okay?" she asked as she fiddled with the leads for another few moments before taking her hand off me and searching through the drawers for something.

I watched as the numbers on the machine instantly started to fall. She turned back to me and placed her hand on my chest, prepared to replace one of the leads, and the numbers started to climb again. She removed her hand again from my chest and watched as the numbers fell. A soft smirk floated across her lips, and that was when she realized that it was her that was making my heart rate go crazy. Her cheeks flushed and her eyes met mine as she rested her palm against my chest again.

"Perhaps you should stop touching me," I teased, grabbing her hand that was still resting against my chest as she watched the monitor.

She smirked at my comment and rolled her eyes. "Did you at least win your fight?" she asked, studying the injuries on my face. Then she looked at my back and ran her fingers over the bruising that I was sure was already starting to show in my kidney area. The machines started beeping wildly again, and without even waiting for my response, she started writing her notes.

"Why is there is no mention of trauma to the kidney area on the forms?" she asked impatiently.

"There is no mention because I didn't say anything," I grunted as she lightly pressed in the area. "Oh and I won. The other guy looks way worse."

"Well, then I'm glad I'm dealing with you and not him then." She kept her head down and continued making notes, studying the monitor. "Any other areas of injury you're not telling us about?" she questioned, those glass-blue eyes glaring at me.

I was going to say something smart, but when I saw the fire in her eyes, I decided to shut up and just shake my head. I didn't need another fight on my hands tonight.

CHAPTER 2

Katy

I KNEW his type too well: another asshole fighter. Just what I needed to come across tonight. I let out a breath and continued writing my notes, making sure to note the bruising in the kidney area. "Are you sure there is nothing else you aren't telling us?" I questioned.

"That's it," he murmured.

I let out a sigh and made note of the bruising along the kidney area. The last few months of my life had been the worst. I had spent all my time plotting my escape from my roid-raged, driven, power-lifting boyfriend, Jonas. However, since I had now made an official getaway, that would now make him my ex-roid-raged, driven, power-lifting boyfriend. The ex part felt great to say and was a pretty big deal to me. I needed to have him long gone and out of my life for good. I shook my head as I took another look at Derrick's swollen face, the cut above his eye starting to concern me. It was deep and swollen and beginning to bruise. It would probably be hard to stitch up, if the doctor didn't get up here soon. I made a few more notes on his chart.

The man who sat across from me was attractive, or would be attractive if his face wasn't swollen shut, but I needed to stop making the same mistakes over and over again. There was no doubt in my mind that this guy would turn out to be exactly the same as my ex. Loving to start off with, and then turn into a monster a few months later.

Derrick had bruises all over him, and judging from the chart that I had briefly perused at the nurses' station, he was a regular in here. That alone screamed at me to not even think about going there with him. He probably also suffered a long list of similar problems to my ex and would be just another huge mistake on an already long list that I would end up wishing I hadn't made.

He cleared his throat, causing me to jump. "I'm an MMA fighter, in case you are wondering. Not just some dick who just likes to pick fights."

It was as if he could read my mind, while I sat there making more notes, practically ignoring him. I could feel his gaze on me while I continued to write. I nodded, half listening as I continued to monitor his vitals.

"I fight for a living. It's what I do. Not a hobby." It was as if he were defending himself to my unsaid thoughts.

"Okay, I got it," I mumbled. I didn't care. Okay, well, that wasn't entirely true. I didn't want to care, because caring only led to me to getting involved with these assholes and getting hurt in the end.

He struggled a bit to sit up, his face flinching in pain, to explain to me. "It's my job. It's my job to fight, sweetheart. It's how I support myself."

"And this is my job, to fix people like you, and please don't call me sweetheart," I said, sounding as cold as I possibly could, continuing to make more notations on his chart. "The doctor will be in shortly. Stay and rest." I pressed a bunch of buttons on the machines, grabbed his chart, and stepped out of the room. I took a deep breath. I didn't need him to sway me. I didn't need him to make me feel anything different than what I already felt. I needed to keep it in my mind that, in the end, he would be nothing but trouble, and I would be fine on my own.

I made my way back to the nurses' station and sat down in my chair, took a sip of my lukewarm tea, and began updating his chart.

"I see you met Dagger," Mollie said, sliding into her chair beside me and signing into her computer. "What do you think? You know, just for the record, he's pretty hot when he isn't all banged up," she said, bumping my arm. "You should totally go for him, that way I can live vicariously through you."

"Who?" I asked, frowning as I continued making notes on my computer and popping some popcorn into my mouth. I couldn't recall a patient by that name, and I was pretty good with names.

She pointed to the closed door across from the desk. "Only the hottest guy here: the MMA fighter, Dagger. Bet he'd be dynamite in the sack."

"Right. Derrick."

Mollie let out a laugh. "Yes Derrick," she mimicked. "You better get used to him. He is here all the time, practically twice monthly. He pretty much recovers from one fight just in time to get into the next one. He says he's working his way up to the big matches. I'll hate to see him after one of those. I've watched some of those fights on TV —broken bones, bruised organs, the trauma to the body is just unbelievable."

"Cool," I mumbled, stuffing a couple more pieces of popcorn into my mouth and making more notes for the doctor. I really didn't want to talk about him. Each and every one of these guys were the exact same, and I had vowed I wouldn't get involved with another one of them. I just hoped she caught on before I snapped at her. I was feeling overly sensitive about this tonight, but I couldn't help it.

"He's really a good guy, Katy," she murmured. "Give him a chance. Maybe he will grow on you."

"What, like a fungus?" I grumbled. It wasn't her fault. She didn't know what I had been through, because I had told no one, and truthfully, I wanted to keep it that way. I had enough people in my life feeling sorry for me; I didn't need the new ones that I met to feel that way too.

She let out a laugh but quieted down instantly when two of the doctors rounded the corner and looked over our way. We were, after all, in an area with some very ill people. It was hardly the time for outbursts of loud laughter.

"He's had a rough childhood, and he turned his anger into something positive. It's a great thing, turning a negative into a positive."

I whipped around. "My God, enough. You sound like an advocate for him or something. A guy who beats up other guys for a living just because he is filled with some sort of rage because he had a rough childhood doesn't sound like a good guy to me. There are many ways to deal with those feelings, starting with a licensed therapist," I snapped at her. I couldn't help it. My ex was the same way, always crying that he'd had an abusive childhood. It still didn't give him the right to treat me the way he had. I knew the type like I knew the back of my hand, and I'd sworn to myself that once I was out of that relationship, I would never get involved with another one of those guys again.

I looked up and over at Mollie, her eyes falling to the ground. "I'm sorry, Katy!" She turned her attention quickly to her computer, ignoring me, a sad look coming over her face. I hadn't meant to, but I had totally snapped. She just didn't know what she was talking about, nor what I had dealt with over the last few years. I was just about to lean over and apologize to her for ripping her one when the doctor I had been waiting for came walking around the corner.

"All right, Katy, let's go and see Dagger, shall we," he said, tapping his thumb on the counter in front of me.

I rolled my eyes. "Et tu, Brute?"

He smirked. "Yes."

I glanced to Mollie, who feverishly typed away on the computer in front of her, and then followed the doctor as he entered the room first. I held the chart in my hand, ready to make any notes as he told me.

"How are you feeling, Dagger?" he asked, stepping up to him, shaking his hand, and looking him over.

"As good as can be expected, doc, and you?"

"I'm well. So, tell me, what happened this time?" he asked as he put on a pair of gloves and took an alcohol swab to the gash above his eye, causing Derrick to flinch.

"This guy snuck up on me. It was a no-good dirty move and the ref called him on it, but the damage was already done, which was what he was pretty much counting on."

I watched as the doctor dropped the little alcohol swab into the garbage and started palpating the middle of his back. "How does this feel?" he asked, pressing into the kidney area.

Derrick sucked in a breath. "Fuck, doc, what do you think? It hurts like hell."

As soon as the doctor removed his hands from the bruised area, Derrick looked at me and smirked. "You're wildly impressed with my pain tolerance, right?" He tried to wink, but with his eyebrow held together with the butterfly sutures that had been put on earlier, it didn't go too well. He laughed. "Hang on, let me try that again." He turned to the other side of his face and tried again.

The doctor let out a loud laugh. "Stop it or I'll have to call in the plastic surgeon on duty, and I already know you hate that guy."

"Please," I murmured under my breath.

Derrick looked at me and then back to the doctor. "That's only because he charges too much and looks like a pretty boy. I can't trust a pretty boy, doc."

The doctor pouted as if he were hurt, and I rolled my eyes again at their banter. "You trust me. Am I not pretty?"

"You, doc? you're ruggedly handsome. And her." He jerked his thumb at me. "She is like girl-next-door gorgeous." He sighed and shook his head. "She has a great bedside manner too; a touch so gentle it's almost like silk. It's too bad she hates me."

The doctor leaned in toward Dagger and looked at me from the corner of his eye. "Don't get your hopes up. You're not special. She hates everyone, even me. Isn't that right, Katy?"

I smirked. The doctor was right... on some level.

CHAPTER 3

Dagger

SHE DIDN'T NEED to say anything else. I could tell from the way she glared at me while the doctor examined me that she definitely hated me. However, I was glad and a bit relieved to know that she basically hated everyone and that it wasn't anything truly personal. In her eyes, I was nothing special, just some loser who fought people, and I could tell she thought that just by the way she looked at me. However, a part of me wondered, even hoped, that maybe I could be special to her if I played my cards right. I already felt she could be special to me if she would let me near her long enough.

As the doctor continued examining me, I stretched and grinned at her as I flinched, every muscle in my body aching. "All right, well, let's get this stitched up, and then you can be on your way to see your next patient, and I can be on my way home to rest. That way I'll leave Nurse Gloom here alone and let her move on to her next case." I smiled.

I glanced over her way, looking to see if that comment had softened her even the tiniest little bit, but she had her face buried in my chart, studying it, ignoring us and waiting for any instructions from the doctor, doing everything and anything she possibly could not to look my way. I couldn't blame her, to be honest. I was an utter mess, but underneath the swollen eye, cut eyebrow, bruised cheek, and fat lip, I was a damn good-looking man.

"That all sounds great, Dag, but first I want an ultrasound of your kidneys. I want to make sure they are, in fact, just bruised, and nothing worse. You've been hit pretty hard back there on more than one occasion. I'm sure you already know that you can expect to pee blood for the next two or three days. However, you know the drill: any longer than that and I want you back in here." The doctor turned to make sure Nurse Grumpy Pants was listening.

I looked over and studied her badge. "Katy, nice name. I like it," I said, wincing as the doctor pressed on the bruise over my lower rib cage to make sure my ribs weren't broken.

"Perhaps an X-ray of his ribs too, both sides, Katy."

Katy continued ignoring me and kept writing. "Anything else, doctor?" she asked, tilting her head to the side, exposing the soft skin of her neck to me. Something about that fascinated me, and I wondered what it would be like to kiss her right there, on that bit of exposed collarbone. I wondered what types of noises she would make as my lips skated over her skin.

The room got quiet and I tore my eyes from her, looking over to where the doc stood. He sat there smirking at me. He knew exactly what I was thinking. Instantly, I felt like a kid who had just been caught looking at a skin mag. He knew. Of course, he did. Out of all the times I had been in this emergency room, this was the hottest nurse I had ever seen; there was no question. There was no doubt in my mind that he was even attracted to her, I thought to myself.

My suspicions were confirmed when she stood up and began getting the tray ready to sew up my face and the doctor's eyes landed directly on her ass.

I swallowed hard and looked away as the doctor finished giving his orders. I guess I had no choice but to wait it out until all the testing was done.

He turned to me and asked me all the usual questions —allergies, health history. Once he was finished, Katy sat down across from me. I did my best not to act as if I were interested in her while she sat there and began really cleaning the wound about my eye, while the doctor started filling out the requisition forms for the X-rays.

"I'm not hurting you am I?" she asked softly as she continued dabbing.

I looked her in the eyes, those glass-blue eyes peering back at me. It was suddenly hard for me not to think those thoughts that had been running through my mind all night.

"It's good, I'm good. Just do what you have to do," I whispered, her eyes still locked with mine.

The doctor cleared his throat behind her and she started cleaning the wound again. I swallowed hard and looked away.

"Dagger! I heard you were in here," the pretty boy plastic surgeon said as he flew through the curtain and into the room, causing Katy to jump and look over her shoulder at him.

"Geez, you're pretty popular around here, aren't you," Katy murmured under her breath as she returned to cleaning my wound. I glanced down at her, her eyes darting away from mine.

"Figured I would come up and see if you wanted me to stitch up your face instead, before this guy here keeps you from that very promising modeling career that you've got lined up later on in life. Those brands will find you, so you're going to need to stay on my good side, you know, to keep you from getting cauliflower ears." He laughed. "And you are welcome," he said, using this singsong voice that had me wanting to poke my eardrums out. Then I saw the way his eyes roamed over Katy as she stood and began to get the sutures ready, and instantly I imagined doing things to pretty boy that wouldn't leave him looking so pretty.

Katy sat back down in front of me and we both exchanged a brief look. At least I knew I hadn't imagined it. From the look she gave me, she didn't like that pretty boy plastic surgeon any more than I did. I watched as his eyes continued washing over her, planting firmly on her ass, and I was beginning to wonder if he was here to take care of her instead of me.

The doctor who was writing up the requisition for me excused himself for a moment and left the room to get something, and that was when pretty boy stepped in.

"So, Katy, what do you say? How about Friday night we go for dinner and then see a movie? There are some great classics playing at the theatre downtown."

She looked me in the eyes, almost pleading with me to save her, then she turned to him. "I don't think so. I have plans," she mumbled.

"So blow them off. I promise to make it worth your while," he said, running his hand over her shoulder and letting it linger there a little longer than I liked.

I watched as she flinched and moved out from under his touch, taking her gloves off. She nodded at me. "I'll be right back." She excused herself and was almost out of the room when pretty boy started to follow her.

"The lady said no," I said loud enough for them both to be sure to hear me. Katy turned and looked over her shoulder at me, a soft smile coming to her lips before she continued on her way.

Just as pretty boy was about to say something to me, the other doctor walked back in, and the tension in the air washed away immediately. The two doctors began talking and ignoring me while I waited for Katy to come back.

I looked past them to the nurses' station and watched Katy as she spoke to Mollie. She rolled her eyes and looked back toward my room, then stopped talking while Mollie said something to her. Maybe she had decided she had been too eager to judge me. At least that was what I hoped had happened. For whatever reason, I really wanted her, of all people, to think that I was a better person than what I was. I really wanted her attention, every ounce of it.

CHAPTER 4

Katy

WITHIN THE HOUR, Dagger had been sent down for his ultrasound and X-rays, and I had completed the remainder of the rounds with the doctor and had just sat down behind the nurses' station with a fresh cup of hot tea. I took a sip, allowing the hot liquid to warm me, and took some time to update the charts in the computer system while it was quiet. I hated more than anything to be behind on my paperwork and always did my best to make sure I remained caught up throughout my shift.

I sat there typing my notes, listening to Mollie talking with one of the other nurses about Derrick. I couldn't help but eavesdrop on them, and judging from what they were saying about Derrick, I could tell every one of them here had something for him. I continued listening to them as they told stories back and forth of the last few times he had been in, and I smiled to myself. They were being ridiculous, acting like teenage girls drooling over some rock star, instead of the married women they were.

A noise to my left distracted me and I spotted Phil, the plastic surgeon. He was back and busy speaking with one of the other doctors on call. I tried to keep my head down and myself busy, but he turned his head in time to catch me watching them. As soon as his eyes met mine, he parted ways with the other doctor and made his way towards me. I smirked when I thought back to how Derrick had stood up for me earlier. It was so sweet how he spoke up after I had left the room. Perhaps the girls were right, and Derrick wasn't all that bad after all.

I let out a sigh. That revelation made me angry with myself. I hated that I was thinking that about him already. This was exactly how I got myself into trouble. It always started with me second-guessing myself and giving people who never deserved it a chance.

"Dagger back yet, Katy?" I turned to see Phil standing behind me.

I cleared my throat and took a sip of tea. "No, sir," I answered, trying to maintain my professionalism.

"Sir? You can call me Phil. I came back because I wanted to check on those stitches."

"Why? Dr. Kent is perfectly capable of stitching in a straight line, as am I." At least Derrick and I seemed to have similar views on things, like this pig of a plastic surgeon.

"I'm sure he is." He reached into my bag of popcorn and took a handful and leaned up against my desk. "Do me a favor and at least think about Friday night, okay," he said, winking at me. "I promise you'll enjoy yourself." He placed his hand on my shoulder, giving me a gentle squeeze. I was just about to ask him to remove his hand when I heard someone call his name, and the next thing I knew, he was walking away.

"What was all that about?" Mollie asked, rushing over to sit down across from me. She watched as Dr. Pretty Boy left the area.

"Nothing." I shook my head, keeping my mouth shut, and returned to my paperwork.

"Could have fooled me. Looks like Phil was getting pretty cozy with you."

"I'm not interested, so he can go and bug someone else," I mumbled, ending the conversation.

Our resident plastic surgeon seemed to be completely interested in both Derrick and me for totally different reasons. He didn't need to see Derrick's stitches, and he didn't need to see me Friday night, that much I was sure of. He was getting plenty of play, I was sure of it. Out of all the nurses here, I was pretty much the only one he hadn't dated at one time or another. If he thought word didn't get around the hospital, he was wrong.

Plus, I knew for a fact that some of the nurses here

would be perfectly happy never having to work another day in their life. He should go after those ones because I was determined to never have to depend on another person for financial support ever again. I had been down that road, and look where it had gotten me. I was being forced to start over, and there really was no security in that. It was all just smoke and mirrors, so he'd better learn, and learn fast, that he was sniffing around the wrong woman.

"Katy, Dagger is on his way back up. I put a stat on that ultrasound and X-ray reports. Let me know as soon as it's in," Dr. Kent said, standing up from the station across from me. "I'm just going to check on rooms five and six, then go on my lunch. You can reach me on my pager if you need."

"Did you need me for anything?"

"Nope, go ahead and continue your paperwork" Dr. Kent had just walked into room five when Dagger rounded the corner. My eyes met his and he tapped the desktop in front of me with his finger, smiled at me, and went back into the room he had been occupying. I couldn't help but catch a glimpse of his rock-hard abs as he reached up and pulled the curtain across the doorway.

"You may want to wipe the drool off your chin." Mollie giggled from across the way.

I jumped and quickly put my head back into my computer and began typing.

Forty minutes later, Derrick's results had come in, and

the doctor returned just as I went to page him. "Derrick's results are in," I said, handing them to him to review.

He glanced down at the reports, quickly looking them over. "Good, only bruising, nothing's broken," he murmured as he sat, continuing to read them over. "Well, let's go deliver these results to Dagger, shall we? Then I'll write up the discharge orders, and you can get started processing those while I check in on rooms one and two."

I nodded and followed the doctor back into the room.

When we entered the room, Dagger was lying back, his arms laced behind his head, staring at the ceiling. As I looked over at him, I caught another quick glance of his bare abs. I could see the tiny trail of hair going down into his pants and felt myself blush as his eyes caught mine. This was ridiculous. I saw naked men all the time in my career; one happy trail was no different than the other.

"Dagger, good news. It's all just bruising. We've been through this before, so I know you know what to expect. Do you have any questions for me?"

Derrick looked at him. "No, doc, we're good. As you said, if I pee blood longer than two or three days, I'll be back."

I was still staring at his exposed abs, the little trail of hair that led down into the front of his pants, and his deeply carved 'V' causing me to continue thinking completely inappropriate thoughts, when he turned his eyes on me. Dagger cleared his throat, and the doctor handed me his chart.

"Katy, notes," Dr. Kent said, holding the chart in front of me, pulling my attention away.

I took the chart from the doctor and looked over at Derrick. As soon as our eyes locked, I saw a smirk settle on his lips and I turned away. No way in hell was I going to be lured in by those big, dark-chocolate brown eyes. I also wasn't going to offer him even a hint of encouragement, although I may have already done that.

"All right, Katy, let's go and get started on Dagger's discharge papers, shall we?"

I nodded and turned to follow the doctor back to the desk where he scribbled down some notes and a couple prescriptions before walking away. Once I had everything, I began the discharge process.

Thirty minutes later, I returned to the room with papers for Derrick to sign and the prescriptions and directions in my hand.

I walked into the room, and the overhead light was now off; just the small wall light on. I found Dagger lying on the table, sound asleep, his one arm still stretched up behind his head, the other flung over his eyes to block out what little light was on in the room. He was lightly snoring away, and as I stood there watching him, I almost didn't want to wake him up. He didn't look restful, though, despite what he had showed earlier. Now I could see the pain he was feeling etched across his face. He wore a bit of a frown, and his jaw was set tightly, his forehead beaded in sweat. Seeing him this way made him seem different, not as hard and much more human. Why hadn't he asked me for pain killers, I wondered.

"Derrick," I murmured in hopes that I would wake him without me having to touch him, but it was just my luck, he didn't even so much as flinch. I stepped a little closer and tried again, this time saying his name just a little bit louder, but again nothing. His breathing didn't even change, so I knew he was out. I stepped closer to the table and placed my hand on his chest, gently shaking him. "Derrick," I whispered.

Without warning, the arm that was covering his eyes came down and his hand landed over top of mine. His large hand enveloped my small one, holding it in place on his hard, muscular chest. "Hmm, yeah, baby? What is it?"

I felt a funny feeling in the pit of my stomach at his soft words and his touch.

Even though I realized he must be dreaming, I stood there for a second, not knowing what to do or say, just taking in the feeling of his warm, hard chest under my hand, his rough, strong hand on top of mine. His body felt different than Jonas', harder, more defined. Jonas was all watery soft from the roids. Perhaps Derrick was all natural.

"What's wrong, sweetie?" he murmured again.

I quickly pried my hand out from under his, while working hard to ignore how such a big, strong, rough man could have a touch that was so soft, gentle, and warm.

At my quick movement he opened his eyes, then sat

up rather quickly, groaning at the fast movement he made. "You're all set. Here is a prescription for some pain killers, two every four to six hours as needed. I think perhaps you should take a couple now." I shoved the bottle of pills into his hand and stepped off to the side, giving him room.

He looked at the bottle in his hand, reading the label, and then shoved the bottle back into my hand and looked at me. "I won't be needing those. Doc knows I don't poison my body with that shit. A couple of days and I'll be back in the gym, good as new."

"Are you crazy? I can see you're in pain," I said, frowning at him. He had just had the shit kicked out of him and here he was talking about being back in the gym. Even though this made me angry on a personal level, I had to keep my composure professional and I bit back my comment. "You should take them with you, just in case you need them," I said, shoving them back into his hand.

"Sweetheart, it's fine. I have a bunch of them at home from the last time I was here. Never took a single one, and I was worse then than I am now. I'll be good." He took my pen and quickly signed the papers, grabbed his sweatshirt, and left the room, leaving me staring after him with his pills in my hand.

CHAPTER 5

Dagger

T̲ʜᴇ ꜱᴛᴀʟᴇ ᴀɪʀ met my nose as I opened the door to my apartment. I walked in and planted my ass down on the old couch that sat against the far wall, the springs moaning out their displeasure at my weight. It was a shitty couch with holes in the material and stuffing popping out, and if you sat on the center cushion, you would get harpooned with a broken spring.

I leaned my head back against the cushion, and as soon as I closed my eyes, I was brought back to that cute little nurse in her purple scrubs, Katy. I hadn't been able to stop thinking about her since I had left the hospital, and as I sat there, I shook my head to try and erase thoughts of her.

Deep down I knew I wasn't good enough for someone

like her. Who did I think I was kidding? I could barely take care of myself, never mind adding anyone else into the mix, but sadly, I could easily see myself falling for her.

Over the years, I'd had my share of pickups, and I was regularly hit on by the ring girls, but I'd not had a steady girlfriend in years. However, I was adamant, there was no way I would date one of them. Those girls were only looking for someone to support them, and when the winning stopped and the money ran out, they would be onto their next guy. I knew it; I saw it every time one of them spoke to me after winning a fight, and since that was the only time they were after me, it just proved I was right. The only thing they saw was that I would be lining my pocket at the end of the night. Five grand was a lot of money for only fifteen minutes in a ring. If that was the payout here in a small town, I could only imagine the payout in one of the bigger cities, and that was why I was working towards Vegas.

I looked around my place. I was living in a shithole, and before I took on the responsibility of looking after and supporting someone else, I needed to find another place, another job, something with more stability. All the money I made in these matches paid for rent, my car, food, gym membership and training so I could keep up my physique. I barely had anything left over at the end of the month after my entry fees were paid up for the next fight.

I let out a sigh. The problem was fighting and working out was all I knew and it would be hard to find something else. At one point I'd thought about maybe coaching kids in schools, perhaps an after school program. I would be able to turn something bad into good, have kids put all the frustration and rage that they carry around to good use. I started to doubt myself when I started wondering if parents would want their child to be taught how to fight. Life today was supposed to be gentler, kinder, and with my luck, I would just be teaching this next generation of children how to bully.

I pulled my phone from my pocket and glanced at the screen. Five new messages were waiting for me. I listened to each one; most of them were my friends congratulating me on my win. The last one was from my trainer. He had been the one to take me to the hospital, dropping me outside the emergency room doors, leaving me there to take a cab home. I figured he would be back on me right away, wondering if I'd be back in the gym in the morning. He saw the fight, he knew the extent of my injuries, but he also knew I was tougher than that. There was no way I was going to let a couple of bruises and ten stitches knock me down.

I rested my head back on the couch and stared up at the stained ceiling. Would I be back in the gym tomorrow? I wanted to be, yet I also never wanted to be there again because I had realized something tonight when I had been looking at that cutie, who stitched my eyebrow so gently I had barely felt a thing. I realized that this job was clearly going to prevent me from having the kind of woman I really wanted for the rest of my life. I wanted someone soft, loving, and caring, and no woman would put up with having her husband or boyfriend beaten to a pulp every couple of weeks. I let out a breath, debating on what to tell him, and dialed his number.

"Dagger, how are you feeling? I take it I will see you at six thirty sharp?" his voice boomed over the phone, loud music playing in the background. No doubt he was either at a club or celebrating the win with one of the ring girls.

I closed my eyes and rested my head on the pillow behind me. I really just wanted one day off, just one, and debated telling him that. My body hurt, and I was tired. I just wanted to sleep, but for some reason I knew if I told him that, he would never let me have that one day off. I could already hear it in his voice. He would also tell me that winners don't quit and give me the same lecture he'd already given me about making it to Vegas.

"Dag?"

"Yeah, man, can we meet for seven instead of six-thirty?" I questioned, closing my eyes and praying he said yes.

"Sure, sure, see you then. Don't be late, and get some rest. I need my star in top shape."

I hung up the phone and threw it down on the couch beside me, rubbing my face. He needed his star in top shape, then he should have given me the day off. He had never let me have the day off before. I didn't know why I would ever think now would be different. He never took pity on me, but if he did, what kind of coach would he be?

I'd have never gotten back in the ring after my first fight, if he'd had any sort of sympathy. I was almost positive he was afraid, scared that if I had a day off here or there, I might find something else to do with my life. He probably felt he needed to keep me on the hook. After all, he wasn't wrong—I was his best fighter. Little did he know, I was already good and hooked. I had to be because I had no other skills to support my sorry ass. What else would I do, be a bouncer? I had tried that a few years ago and had many guys wanting to try me every night once they got booze into them. I didn't drink and got tired of that scene quick, not to mention the money was shit. I'd never be able to support myself on that kind of money.

I let out a large yawn and stretched, but stopped when the pain started shooting through the middle of my back. Fuck I needed sleep. I glanced at the clock. It was almost two, and I was in pain and exhausted. There was nothing else for me to do but sleep because before I knew it, it would be time to get up and head into the gym. I needed rest bad, not only to heal, but to be ready for tomorrow. If not I would find myself paired with a shitty sparring partner who didn't care I had just won my last fight, and I wouldn't get better sparring with someone who was awful. He would just want to beat the shit out of me, a guy who already looked like he had been beaten because I would look like an easy target. I didn't need a partner like that. I needed one who would help me grow as a fighter.

I got up from the couch and walked over to the bed,

dropped my sweatpants and T-shirt on the floor, and flopped down on the weak mattress. As soon as my head hit the pillow, I was out. It felt as if I'd been asleep for hours when I woke with a start, and at first, I thought I had slept past my gym time. When I realized I hadn't, I lay there staring up at the ceiling thinking about what had woken me. I'd had a dream that I had finally gotten myself out of this hellhole and was living in a decent, clean place. I wasn't fighting anymore, and I was on my way to pick up my girl.

As I approached the door to her place and knocked, I felt a funny feeling inside me, perhaps excitement, right down deep in the pit of my stomach. When the door opened, Katy stood staring back at me, a soft smile on her face and the look of love in her eyes. That look had jarred me awake. The nurse who hated me in real life was the girl in my dreams, the one I was with, and suddenly I felt the letdown hit, because that would never happen; she was too good for a guy like me. I let out a little laugh and rolled over, shrugging it off.

I guess a guy could dream.

CHAPTER 6

Katy

I DRESSED in my favorite pair of jeans and hooded sweat-shirt and pulled my wet hair back into a makeshift pony-tail. It had been a long night and I was practically dragging myself from the changing room. My duffel bag was heavy, full of dirty scrubs from the week and two towels. Letting it hang from my shoulder, I made my way to the employee's only door of the hospital. Over the last couple of years, I had forgotten how long and draining hospital shifts really were. Twelve hours straight of whatever came through those emergency room doors. You never knew hour to hour or minute to minute what you would be faced with, and to be honest, I was afraid I didn't have the energy to deal with it anymore. I guess I had gotten soft over the last little while.

Before starting here I was working for a doctor's office, working straight days, eight to five, with weekends and holidays off. I was spoiled most of the time with hour-long lunches with no interruptions and two fifteen-minute breaks. I was hardly ever attached to a pager or a cell phone, unless there was an emergency. The best part of those days was getting to sleep at night, all night long, and being able to have a life on weekends with my friends. Now I was lucky to be able to get a lunch or a break, as most of them now were spent eating popcorn and drinking tea while I did up patient reports, so I didn't fall behind.

I pushed the door open and stepped out into the early-morning air. I walked to my car and thought back to those days, remembering how happy I had been. That job had even paid well enough for me to save up and buy my own house, all by myself. My friends and I had even gone out to celebrate my purchase, and it was shortly after that everything began to change.

My friends started dating, some got married, and then they began having families. At that time, I was so happy for them, and even though they made sure they included me on all holidays, I was beginning to feel alone. My social life was dwindling down to nothing, and I found myself with this odd want to find a guy. You'd think it would have been easy, since I worked in a large medical office. I could have my pick of any type of doctor I wanted, surgeon, specialist, but I had made a pact with myself never to mix my work life with my personal life; things got to messy. So instead, I turned to one of my friends. She set me up with her boyfriend's friend, John, and I had reluctantly agreed to a date the following weekend after Michelle's bachelorette party. That date never happened because that was the night my life changed. It was the night I meant Jonas.

We were on the dance floor at a local bar when he caught my eye. I had seen him around town numerous times before, but I had never spoken to him, and in retrospect, I probably should have left it that way.

He was sitting over in a booth against the far wall, feet up on the seat, drink in hand, intently watching me, or as my friend said "eye-fucking the shit out of me." I had done my best to ignore him, trying not to glance in his direction and encourage him, but I was a sucker for muscles, and he had muscles.

When the song we had been dancing to was over, Michelle and I headed back to our group. As I walked away, I had glanced over my shoulder and met his eyes. There was something about the way his eyes washed over my backside that I loved. When we got back to our table, Jen brought over our next round of drinks and handed me my cherry cooler, and that was when I heard a man clear his throat behind me.

"Ladies, could my friends and I buy you a shot?" I felt a hand land on my shoulder.

I rolled my eyes at Jen; she knew how much I hated

guys like this. She hit me in the arm, and I turned to see the guy who had been watching me earlier, his intense, dark eyes staring back at me.

"What are you ladies celebrating?" he asked, not taking his eyes off me.

"Our friend here is getting married," Cynthia, one of the girls from across the table, said.

"This friend?" he questioned, pointing to me and squeezing my shoulder. "That sure is a shame." His eyes ran the length of my body again.

"No, not Katy. Katy will never get married. It's Michelle," Jen said, pointing to Michelle, who was busy downing a shot of tequila with Emily.

I locked eyes with the tall stranger, and he flashed me a sexy smile. He stepped up behind me and placed his hands on my upper arms and leaned into my ear. "I'm not even going to begin to tell you how happy it makes me to hear you aren't the one getting married."

I smiled back and looked into his dark eyes. "Why is that?" I asked, taking a drink of my cooler.

"Because then I wouldn't have the chance to date such a beautiful angel."

My stomach did a somersault at his words. I had never been spoken to like that before, and for the rest of the night, he hung around, buying me drinks and dancing.

By the end of the night, my friends had talked me into accepting a date with him. I had canceled my date with John Thursday night, and that Friday night I spent time with Jonas in his garage watching him work on his muscle car while listening to music. The night ended with us ordering takeout and binging a show on Netflix. We fell into bed the following weekend and started dating shortly after that. He was amazingly thoughtful and gorgeous. Even a bunch of girls from work wondered how I had landed such an amazing looking guy. They were right, he had a body of a god, but he should have for the amount of time he spent in the gym. Soon we were spending all our time together, and soon I had fallen completely head over heels for him.

Everything was great, but in hindsight, I should have paid way more attention to what was really going on. There were nights I would come home from work and head over to his place to find his apartment completely destroyed. His temper was not one to mess with, and he would fly off the handle at almost anything. He was pushy and demanding, and I, for whatever reason, was desperate enough to believe his lies and excuses when he apologized.

Soon he was controlling my every move, denying me nights out with co-workers and friends because he claimed he needed me. It hadn't taken me long to finally figure out what was going on. His mood swings were courtesy of the steroids; he was juicing, but I was in denial and had completely misread the situation. Now it was too late.

Our first big fight came on a Tuesday afternoon. We were supposed to be going out with some of his friends after I was done working. However, I was running late. I had to wait for some blood results to come back from the lab for one of our patients. The doctor had asked me to stay until the fax came in and send him a text as soon as I received it. Forty-five minutes after we had closed, the fax had finally come in. I knew I was already in trouble with Jonas, so I quickly sent the doctor a snapshot of the report, locked the office, and made my way to Jonas' apartment. As soon as I walked through the door he came at me.

"Where the fuck you been?" he growled.

"Sorry, I told you I had to wait for a report to come in. A patient needed her results today," I said, flinging my purse onto the table and trying to ignore the fact that he was in a rage.

"That's the fucking doctor's job, Katy, not yours. When you tell me you're going to be home at a certain time, you fucking need to be here. What's going on, does that rich prick have his dick inside of you? Your pussy getting bored with me!" he shouted, grabbing me and pushing me up against the wall.

I was shocked at his outburst, and when I didn't respond, he smashed his fist through the wall just inches from my face. I fought back tears as he let me go and continued slamming things around the apartment, stomping and barking. Instead of collecting my belongings and leaving like I should have done, I let what had just happened go and got ready. I figured he was just angry at the situation. What I didn't want to see was he was really a controlling and abusive boyfriend in the making. Somehow, as these incidents continued, I felt like I deserved being treated like that.

Things calmed down for a while, and soon he had apologized and things went back to normal, but it didn't last long. Two weeks later, I was busy studying for an upcoming exam I needed to take, and I accidentally burned dinner. That was the night he hit me for the first time. Instantly, I snapped back at him, causing him to hit me again. The second time he hit me, only a week later, we were getting ready for Michelle's wedding. He didn't want to go, but I didn't want to have to explain to everyone where he was. After he beat me, I changed my dress to hide the already forming bruises that he had left on my arms, and instead of staying for the entire evening, we made an appearance at the ceremony and I faked sick. He, of course, put on a great show, acting as if he actually cared about me, which my friends ate up.

Two weeks after that was the first time he actually hit me in the face. It was a Monday morning and he had already left for the gym. I stood in the bathroom wrapped in a towel, my arms and upper body black and blue. I stared at my right eye; it was completely bloodshot from the hit, and it was already starting to turn that beautiful shade of black and blue.

My stomach did flips as I glanced at the clock. It was already seven. I had to be at work in an hour and I had no way to hide this. Bruises on my arms, chest, legs, and back could be easily hidden with long sleeves and pants, but the face? There was no way I could do anything about my face. I'd seen plenty of young girls come into the clinic wearing globs of makeup to hide the bruises their boyfriends had left for them. I couldn't do the same.

That morning I walked into the office with my sunglasses on and sat down behind the desk and started in on e-mails. Eric came out from his office.

"Morning, Katy. Do you have Mrs. Sullivan's file?" he asked, pouring himself a cup of coffee and turning to look at me.

I quickly handed him the file, praying he didn't notice I still had my sunglasses on.

He cleared his throat. "Um, Katy, you forgot to take your sunglasses off, silly girl."

"Oh geez, I didn't realize," I said, staring at the computer screen. "I have a bad headache today," I lied.

He stood there looking at me. "Well? You can't see patients like that today."

I slid the glasses off my face, careful not to look at him, and put them in my purse. I couldn't see patients anyways with the shiner I had.

"Katy, could I see you in my office for a second?" he asked.

I nodded, closed my eyes, and followed him into his office.

He sat down behind his desk, gesturing for me to take the seat across from him. "Katy, what is going on?"

I tried to play dumb. "What do you mean?" I asked, swallowing hard.

"Katy, look at yourself. I've worked with you for a long time. I've never seen you looking so..." he hesitated. "I've noticed the bruises, Katy. I'd have to be an idiot not to, and now the black eye," he sighed. "I don't want to have to do this, but I have no choice. I can't have you coming into work looking like this. You need to get out of this relationship. I'm going to give you a week off. You need to get home and get out of this. If you need help, I can get you help; there are programs."

I had envisioned this exact moment and I swore I would be stronger than I ended up being, but as the words fell from his mouth, a tear slipped from my eye and down my cheek. I quickly wiped it away. He was right.

I gathered my things after our conversation and made my way back to my house. Only when I returned, Jonas was there, working out in the garage with two other guys I didn't recognize. I didn't want to fight about why I was back home, so I just told him I wasn't feeling well and went in and crawled into bed.

Soon the eye healed, I stayed out of trouble with Jonas, and I went back to work. I didn't tell Eric that I was still in the relationship. I lied and told him I had gotten out of it because there was no way I could have left without getting hurt. Instead, every chance I got I planned and planned, and it took me another six months of planning before I had decided to run.

A blaring horn quickly reminded me that I was in the parking lot of the hospital, and I jumped back as they drove by. It was cool this morning, and a shiver ran through me as I walked quickly through the parking lot to my car. I unlocked the door of my car and threw my duffel bag into the back seat. I was convinced I had done a good job of hiding in a big city with a new job at a large hospital. I got into the driver's seat and looked out the windshield and realized that perhaps I hadn't. There, right in my field of vision, was a large handprint sprawled out on the glass.

A funny feeling sank into the pit of my stomach as I put the key in the ignition and looked around the parking lot for any signs of other people. There wasn't anyone around, and I didn't wait. I turned the engine on and as I pulled out from the parking spot, I saw a car's lights start up and pull out of a spot across the parking lot from where I had been parked.

I tried to see who was driving the car but couldn't. I swallowed hard. Perhaps Jonas had found me. I kept watch in my rearview mirror, praying that the car turned off onto another road, and it finally did only a couple blocks from where I was living. If it truly was Jonas, I was going to have to figure out what the hell I was going to do. Until that time, I would just pack up my shit and move again.

CHAPTER 7

Dagger

I TRUDGED across the floor of my apartment to the bath-room for a hot shower, every part of my body aching. I turned the shower on and brushed my teeth while I waited for the water to heat. Pulling the shower curtain back, I stepped in under the hot spray and let the heat from the shower soak into my body just enough for me to feel human again. By the time I was finished, the water had started to turn cold.

I reached for the ratty towel that hung on the towel rack and wrapped it around my waist. I stepped out of the shower just in time to see three cockroaches sitting on the edge of the bathroom sink.

"For fuck's sake," I mumbled under my breath.

Quickly grabbing my gym shoe from the floor, I smashed them, killing all three of them. I leaned against the bathroom sink and looked at myself in the mirror. I was living in such a hole.

I looked at the shower behind me. Tiles were missing on the wall, and two more were just about ready to fall off. I looked down at the sink. It was cracked, and the toilet would continuously run if not flushed carefully.

"Fuck me!" I yelled out.

I marched out of the bathroom, holding the towel around my waist, and grabbed my phone. I'd had enough. I dialed that dick of a landlord and left yet another message on his phone. This was the third time I'd called this month, and he had ignored every single one of them. This time I didn't bother leaving a message. I threw my cell on the bed. I knew he wouldn't call back, but come the first of the month, he would be here to pound on my door, and every other door in this shithole, to collect his four hundred bucks. The fact that he hadn't called me back led me to believe that he had labeled me one of his problem tenants. That meant I was probably on top of the list of the people he needed to evict sometime in the upcoming months, and knowing him, he would take pleasure in telling me to get out.

I threw on my workout shorts and went over to the kitchenette and began to shove handfuls of spinach and broccoli along with a scoop of my protein powder into the blender cup that sat on the counter. I added coconut milk along with a handful of blueberries and raspberries and blended up my breakfast. My head and body still ached, and I seriously doubted that I would be able to make it through my gym session this morning.

I grabbed two ibuprofens from the kitchen cabinet and downed them with my shake, hoping they would dull some of the pain. My hands were swollen, my knuckles red and raw, and I could barely make a fist. Hopefully, they would be fine by the time I started hitting that good ole bag later this morning.

I downed the remainder of my shake and grabbed my bag and keys. With my gym bag slung over my shoulder, I was just about out the door when my phone rang. "Yeah, it's Dag," I barked into the phone.

"Delgado, you do realize that I have a list of people who would be more than willing to take your shithole of an apartment, right?"

As soon as I heard his voice, I rolled my eyes but bit my tongue. Over the years I had always been quick with my replies to anyone who pissed me off, which had ulti-mately been responsible for landing me right where I was today. Instead, I said nothing and just listened.

He was a nothing but a bully. He knew I had nowhere to go and probably wouldn't find anything cheaper. He also knew I couldn't afford to pay any more, and there were many months that I had asked for another week to be able to get him his full rent.

"You know, Delgado, you, my friend, are living in

prime real estate, and I could have your place rented out in a matter of seconds. As a matter of fact, I just got off a call from a very desperate mother. Her and her two kids were practically begging me for a place! Is it time I write up an eviction letter? Spell it all out to you in black and white."

"Fuck you, John," I spat into the phone. "You're a fucking bully." He was just like every other bully I had confronted in my lifetime. They loved to make a person bleed.

I tried to rein in my temper but couldn't. The threat he had spit at me had done it, and I snapped. "I don't live in prime real estate; I live in a fucking efficiency. Do you even know what that means? That means I can sit on the fucking can and brush my teeth at the same time that my feet are in the shower. Did you know it's actually easier for me to treat that short-ass sink as a fucking urinal than it is to use the toilet that it hangs over. Basically, I have to slide myself underneath the sink to take a fucking dump!"

John hadn't had the pleasure of seeing me snap, but now he would. I'd had enough. "Don't come barking around here for your fucking rent either, asshole."

"That's it, Delgado! You're out!"

The phone went silent and it took me a minute to realize he had hung up. I pocketed my phone. I now had plenty of anger and angst in me and knew I needed to work it off. I was also damn determined after my workout to find myself a new place. I was living in fucking Virginia

Beach. Surely there was something here that was better than this filth.

I drove to the gym, thinking about my options. I was determined not to live in my car again. I'd been there and done that, showering in the gym bathroom and using restaurant bathrooms. I needed my life to be different and knew that staying in that hellhole would keep me where I was. So, if for the time being I had to sleep in my car, I guess I could, at least for the remainder of the summer. It would give me time to get a couple of fights under my belt and some money in my pocket for something a little nicer.

"That's it, Dag, keep going. Left, left, left, right," my trainer called from behind the bag.

I was hitting that bag extra hard today, and I was pretty jacked up by the time it came time to spar. I took all my rage out on my poor partner, barely giving him any time or chance to hit me back, finally knocking him to the ground.

I walked back to the changing room, utterly exhausted with ice on both of my swollen hands. My trainer walked with me to my right. I could tell he was impressed with what he had just watched.

"Dag, if only you could fight like that in the ring every single time, no one would ever stand a chance coming up against you."

"Thanks, coach! Frustrations were high!" I took the towel that hung around my neck and wiped the sweat from my brow.

"Let me know what to do to piss you off every time and you'll be golden!" We both laughed.

"Hey, I saw the announcement that came out for the big fight. You think there is a chance you could get me into one of those big matches at the end of next month?"

"Absolutely, I think there's good possibility. Tell you what, you get home, get some rest, and I will look into it and see if I can get you registered," he said, smacking me on the shoulder. "I have to go meet up with my next client."

After I took a long, hot shower, I made my way to the car. I was looking forward to hearing what coach had to say about the big match. I knew he would get me into this fight. I also knew that the recruiters would be there from larger cities.

I drove back to my apartment excited about the opportunity, the windows down and music blaring. I thought to myself that maybe, just maybe, things would start to get better for me, that this was the window of opportunity I needed. The good mood lasted until I pulled into my parking spot outside of my apartment building. I was just in time to see the last bag of my things being deposited to the curb. John dropped it into the pile with the others. That asshole had come and emptied out my apartment.

"What the fuck!" I yelled, beating my hand against my steering wheel, and climbed out of the car, slamming the door. I came around the front of it just in time to see the slimy fucker smile and wave as he sauntered back up the stairs to what was once my apartment.

If I didn't fear going to jail, I would have charged up those stairs and taken a swing at him. I wasn't surprised that guys like this got off on bullying people, and even though I'd clean the floor with him, he wasn't worth it. Instead, I watched after the prick as he climbed the stairs up to my apartment, the anger building in me. *He's not worth it*, I reminded myself as I gathered my things and threw them into the back seat of my car.

I got into my car and drove down the road, stopping at the nearest motel that claimed they had vacancy. The place was a complete dive from the outside anyways, which funnily enough gave me an inch of hope that I just might be able to afford this place, until I could find something else. The good thing was I hadn't paid for this month's rent at the other place yet, so I still had that money. I went into the office and waited at the counter.

"Can I help you?" A man emerged dressed in dirty jeans and a white wife beater, a bottle of beer in his dirty hands.

"I need a room," I mumbled as I counted what money I had in my pocket.

"One day, three, what?" he asked, putting the bottle down and wiping his hands on his jeans before grabbing his register book.

"A month, maybe more."

The man's eyes lit up and he rubbed his hands

together before grabbing a long-term stay sheet. I threw my driver's license on the counter. These guys must love people like me. A full month's worth of rent, and he doesn't have to worry about getting someone in that room nightly. Makes his job easy. Although in this neighborhood, with the room rates what they were, he probably had no trouble with that. The working girls on the street had a place to go, and the sheets were usually clean.

"Did you want the place cleaned daily?" he asked as he copied information off my driver's license.

"Weekly is fine. Are there laundry facilities here?"

"Across the street. That will be two-hundred and fifty dollars."

I gladly paid the man. I could actually afford the cost and had a few dollars leftover in my pocket for some food. I just hoped the place wasn't worse than what I came from. If I had to, I could probably stay two or three more months, until I saved up the money and found a nicer place. At least I would have a roof over my head. I had another fight coming up at the end of the month, and I would have more money in my pocket by then. I got the key and carried the bags from the trunk of my car up to the door that was to be my new home.

I was just about to slide the key into the lock when I heard a woman whistle behind me. "Well, well, what do we have here...hmmm."

I turned around in time to catch a flash of leg and the

top of a breast spilling out of her top before she was almost on top of me.

"You'll be a pleasure to do. I'll give you my special $75 dollars and I'm yours for the night, sugar."

"Not interested, thanks," I said, pushing her off my arm. She flipped me the bird and went off in search of another customer. I needed out of places like this. All the more reason to get on John's ass to get me into these bigger fights. I slid the key into the lock and opened the door.

The stale air that met my face told me that the room hadn't been opened in a while, but it had been cleaned. As I stepped inside I could tell from the looks of things this place was cared for. I dropped my bags onto the floor just inside the door and walked farther inside. As I stepped, it didn't feel like the floor was about to give way like the last place.

I walked into the bathroom and turned the water on and washed away the dried blood on my hands from where they had split open this morning. Even the water pressure here was better than in the last place, and the sink was actually on a vanity. The toilet was beside it. I chuckled to myself and walked back into the room.

The small kitchenette didn't have much to cook with other than a microwave, but I had my hot plate. I opened the small bar fridge and could feel the cool air fall from it and smiled at the fact I wouldn't need to worry about food rotting.

I grabbed the last few bags from my trunk and brought

them inside and opened the two tiny windows on either side of the door before flopping down on the bed. The mattress didn't groan like the last one, and I didn't have springs shooting up into my back. It was actually pretty comfortable. I grabbed the remote and threw the TV on and flipped through the stations. Only fifteen channels, but it was twelve more than I had gotten in my last place.

As I looked around the room, the TV droning on in the background, I finally felt things might be changing. I was moving up in the world, I could feel it. Now all I needed was to secure a spot in the big fight at the end of the next month, get a contract, and head off to the bright lights of the Vegas MMA.

CHAPTER 8

Katy

My heart raced as I lay in bed. The mere thought that it was Jonas' handprint on my windshield had sent me into a tossing, turning fit while I tried to get some sleep. I finally gave up after four hours and got up. All I could concentrate on was packing up and getting out of this place. If he were in fact following me, he could show up at any minute and bang down my door and I wouldn't stand a chance.

I didn't want to take any chances and wash my scrubs at the laundromat, so instead I left them in the bag they had come home with me in and I began to pack the rest of my clothes in my suitcases. Once one was full, I carefully packed the remainder of my things in the other suitcase and spare duffel bag and loaded everything into my car. I quickly ran to the grocery store nearby and got a large box to put the few kitchen supplies I had in it, along with the few items I had bought for the week.

As I continued to pack, I thought about how I had gotten here. I remembered leaving my old town, my pretty little house with the large yard, like it was yesterday. Only it had now been six months; I had been on the run for six months.

My mind quickly flashed back to the day I had made my escape. We'd only had a couple of hours until Jonas returned, so we had to work fast. He had gone to the gym like he did every morning. His workouts were normally two hours, but most days he was gone for three or four. Still, I didn't want to take that chance that today he would come back early and that he would return all jacked up on adrenaline and juice.

I had enlisted the help of my three best friends and their husbands to come and help me pack and load up everything. There was barely enough time with all of us, and since everything in the place belonged to me, which wasn't much, I had decided it was coming with me. While the men loaded the furniture and other heavy items into the U-Haul, us women took care of the little things. Since Jonas had always been around, the only few things I had packed up were the items that were most precious to me and the ones I didn't want broken in one of our fights, wrapped them carefully and placed them into boxes. One night when he had asked me what I was doing, I had lied and told him that I was selling them.

With the help of the girls, my clothing was packed into three large suitcases, while the other packed up the bathroom stuff, and I packed up the kitchen. The whole process took us less than an hour and a half, and with the U-Haul packed, my clothes, toiletries, and a few kitchen supplies packed into the back of my car, we drove off towards the storage facility. I had decided to leave what little food there was in the fridge and the cupboards; I would just get new wherever I settled.

Sarah, who was in real estate, had talked me into renting the place out, which would mean I would have to evict Jonas. She helped me file all the correct documents last week, and she would mail the notice to him after I was gone to make sure I was safe. She said until I decided if I was going to keep the house and move back later, at least I could use the income from the rent as pocket money after the mortgage had been paid.

When we finally pulled up outside the storage facility, Sarah ran in and rented a locker. There was no way I could chance that Jonas might actually check out this place. He wasn't a stupid man, and I needed to protect myself in any and every way I could. Within minutes, Sarah walked out of the main office with a key in hand, and we drove inside the compound and began unloading everything. We weren't halfway finished when my cell-phone rang. With shaky hands, I pulled the phone from my pocket and glanced down at the screen.

"Hi, Helen." I breathed heavily into the phone. "Everything okay?"

"Katy, Jonas just got home." Her voice shook as she spoke, "He went into the house, started shouting, and is now outside in the front yard throwing things around. He has already broken two windows, and I'm pretty sure he may have kicked the door in. Please, please tell me you're safe, honey."

Helen had always been concerned about me. Over the last few months, she had also noticed the bruises on me and had asked me numerous times if he had been hurting me. Of course, I covered for him all the time, until the last time he had beaten me, when I needed immediate help. I had quietly gone out the back door of the house and went to Helen's and waited there until Sarah could get there. Helen knew I was planning to leave today. She also knew if I wasn't gone before Jonas arrived, I probably wouldn't live.

"Thanks, Helen. I'm safe. I'll call the police, but please, whatever you do, do not go outside or open your door if he bangs on it." I hung up the phone and, together with my friends by my side, we quickly made an anonymous call to the police. I feared for Helen, in case he took his rage out on her. They were sending cars right away, and we continued to quickly unload the U-Haul.

I signed over all the final documents Sarah needed to

look after the house, smiled at her, and handed her her pen. I hoped to one day return to it, but with me needing to be so far away, she needed to have full control over what was going on with it.

"All right, bug, you drive as far as you can today and call us when you get there." Paul said, "Sarah and I will take the U-Haul back for you."

I nodded. I was scared to say the least, but I knew I couldn't stay here. Jonas would eventually end up killing me. It would only be a matter of time.

Paul stopped me before I got into the car and handed me a wad of bills. "From us, a little emergency money," he said, shoving it into my hand and kissing my forehead.

I stared down at the bills in my hand. "Guys, I can't take this," I said, shoving the money back at Paul.

"Yes, you can. Now, you'd better go," he said, pulling me in for a final hug.

With tears in my eyes, I climbed into the front seat of the car and placed the cash into my purse. As I drove away, I looked in my rearview mirror to see them all watching and waving as I drove off into the proverbial sunset.

That night I drove as far east as I could, only stopping for coffee, food, and gas. When I could no longer keep my eyes open, that was when I pulled off into a motel hidden in the heart of a little city in the middle of nowhere. I stayed the night, parking my car behind the building, out of sight from the road.

Once in my room, I pulled the curtains tightly closed and not only locked the doors, but also pulled the empty dresser in front of it. That way should Jonas have followed and found me, I would have some kind of warning that he was coming in.

Not much had changed in the past six months as I looked over my shoulder to the door and saw the dresser pulled across it. This had been my life since I had left, hopping hotel to hotel, always looking over my shoulder. It was getting tiring, to say the least.

I felt so defeated. Every time I got comfortable somewhere, clues that he was following me would subtly start to appear. It was as if he were taunting me, giving me clues, biding his time. I couldn't risk staying in one place any longer than a couple of months. As soon as I would see the clues start to appear, I would pack up and move to the next hotel in the area, hoping he wouldn't find me. I really didn't want to start having to search for a new job or start a new life all over again, but if I had to move farther east, I would.

I could feel the panic starting to settle in my chest, making it hard for me to breathe. I sat down on the edge of the bed, taking a quick break and looking around at the scattered mess. All of this was because I had seen a huge handprint on the window of my car.

"You're so stupid. You should have purchased a new car," I mumbled to myself, "not just register this one to the state."

I had made one mistake out of all of this, and that was it, and I'd never let myself live it down. I had been trying to conserve what little money I had, but in hindsight, this was my safety and that should have come first. I took a few deep breaths, grabbed a bottle of coke from my little bar fridge, and took a sip.

I didn't have anyone here who I could turn to for help, and I didn't want to worry my friends back home; they had done enough for me. I also didn't know any of the nurses or doctors at the hospital well enough to ask them for help either. The only one I could say I knew was Mollie, and that was only because she worked right beside me and liked to tell me about all her problems. I hadn't told her any of mine, mainly because I didn't want pity from her or anyone else. I just new that I needed to feel and be safe, and at this moment, I felt none of those things. Honestly, I had no idea if that handprint was even his, but something in my gut told me it was better to be safe than sorry.

My only option was to move. I got back up and continued packing the last few articles of clothing and zipped up the bag, then gathered the remainder of my things. I loaded my suitcases into the back of my car and went back into my room, packing up what little food I had left, along with my hot plate. As soon as it was all in my car, I walked across the parking lot to the main office and checked out of the extended stay. I thanked my lucky stars —well, the few I had—that I only had to pay per week here. That had been part of the appeal of staying here, because I never knew how long I would be able to stay. With only paying a week at a time, if I had to pack up early, I had only wasted money on a couple of days.

I turned over my key and walked back across the parking lot, removing my sweatshirt and throwing it onto the passenger seat. I climbed into my car and opened my Google maps. I searched for another extended stay hotel, finally finding one on the other side of town. It would be farther from the hospital, but it would have to do.

I backed my car out of my parking spot and made my way over to my next home, praying that it was only my imagination and Jonas wasn't really out there looking for me.

CHAPTER 9

Dagger

My body lay half under the covers as I floated in and out of sleep and relished in the quietness of my new place, which was so much nicer than the last place I was in. I would have been woken half a dozen times or so throughout the night with people fighting and screaming at one another. Even though the outside of the place looked like a dive, it was clean and as quiet as a church.

I took a few deep breaths and stretched. Mentally, I felt like a million bucks after an entire week of eight solid hours of sleep a night, but my body was still exhausted. I was always like this when healing up after a fight. I could feel the exhaustion in my body with every fiber of my being, and I knew I had to get up and head to the gym.

That was my routine everyday: gym, errands, home...wherever home may be at that time, and then I would do it all over the next day. Not much changed in my life from day to day.

I sat up and looked around the room. The only thing missing from my life now was a little excitement—of the legal kind, of course—and a good woman. Other than that, I was as happy as I could be with my life, I guess. Less complications and less issues.

Although, like everybody, I had my share of other kinds of issues. Most of them, though, had never truly been mine. They were mostly friends or guys from the gym who had needed advice. I had watched them all make some huge mistakes and ruin their lives and careers over one night of poor choices. All of these decisions came from the pressure in our business, but me? I was going to do it the right way. I planned to stay clean and keep my nose to the ground and stay far, far away from anything or anyone that would steer me the other way. That was also part of the reason I wouldn't date a ring girl. Most of them were so wrapped up in drugs that one slip, one night of partying, and I could easily see my career going down the toilet. That was another reason why I never once faltered off my routine; it kept me out of trouble.

I got up. I had lounged around as long as I could. I went and jumped in the shower, letting the hot water run over my aching muscles. I still had a bit of a backache from the last fight, but I had finally stopped peeing blood a few days ago—a few more days than the doctor had warned me about.

I stood under the spray of the shower, and once the heat got into my muscles and I stopped aching, I shut the shower off and dried, wrapping the towel around my waist. Not only did the hot water last past the end of my shower here, but the towels here were better, I thought to myself.

I grabbed jeans and T-shirt from my bag and threw them on and quickly made my morning workout shake: spinach, broccoli, a few berries, kale, mixed with a couple of scoops of protein powder and water. I downed the green liquid, rinsed my cup, and headed out the door.

I stepped out of the changing room and made my way out to meet my trainer. The gym was busier than normal this morning. I looked around finally spotted him in the corner with another young fighter I hadn't seen before, so I headed over to the warm-up area and started on my own. I began with stretching, and once I was finished, all the stiffness had left my body, then it was on to my warmup. This morning's routine was mostly body weight exercises, push-ups, wall sits, planks, a little balancing on the BOSU, followed by some heavy lifting, and then off to the punching bag. Every hit I delivered to that bag felt great. I still didn't have full range of motion, but my trainer was sure it would be back before I knew it. Then we hit the ring for a quick sparring match.

"Don't show your pain to your opponent, Dag. You got

this. The next big match is in a couple of weeks. You need to be ready," he shouted from the sidelines as the guy I was sparring against punched me in the kidney area, causing me to go down. I was still severely bruised back there, and I called a time out as I breathed through the pain on my hands and knees until it subsided and I could get back up.

"I got it, don't worry," I mumbled as I made my way over to the side of the ring for water. "Fighting while in pain has taught me not to show my weaknesses to my opponents, unless they hit me there right now," I said, squeezing water into my mouth.

"Why do you think I always make you come in, regardless of your condition?"

I nodded. "I know, so I learn." That strength alone had come in handy during many fight nights. He said it was part of my secret, me hiding my weaknesses but learning how to watch for theirs and taking advantage of them when I could. It had been a hard thing to learn, taking time and patience, but it was easier to learn how to do that during practice than it was in the middle of a real match, in a real ring. I owed a lot to my trainer; he was the one who had instilled the good old "Practice makes perfect" mentality in my head when I first started with him, and soon perfect was what I started to achieve during the fights that mattered, the ones that earned me money, and the ones that would further my career.

"You going to be ready for Vegas? The scouts will be

out soon," he said, passing me a towel to wipe the sweat from my brow.

"Does that mean you got me into that match at the end of next month?" I asked.

He nodded. "Yep, just waiting for the confirmation call. You're sure you're going to be ready? There is nothing wrong with waiting another month or two."

"Yep, coach, I'll be ready." Vegas was calling me. I was ready for the big-time matches, where the real money lied.

"All right, I guess that is it for today, Dag. You trained hard today."

I climbed out of the ring, dripping with sweat, and made my way back to the changing room with my trainer.

"You know I am going to want to double your training time."

I nodded. "I'll do whatever it takes to get me to the big leagues, so if it means doubling up on training and fighting in whatever fights necessary to get me there, I'll do it."

"All right, good stuff. As soon as I hear, I'll call!"

I shook hands with my coach and headed to the shower and cleaned myself up. As soon as I had packed up my bag, I headed over to the grocery store. I could only pick up a little bit of food at a time; the little fridge in my room only held so much, but at least it worked. The fridge had crapped out in my last place, and the landlord refused to fix it, causing me to have to eat out.

I wandered through the store picking up the few things I needed and paid for my purchase. Then I made my way over to the health food store. I was out of my protein and had taken the last of my vitamins this morning.

As I left the store, I felt like there was an extra spring in my step. I felt great. I didn't need to worry about roaches or mice getting into my food anymore. Plus, now that I knew the coach had a line on this fight, I felt that my chances at a better life were actually taking form.

With protein powder and vitamins shoved in the bag, I made my way across the parking lot to my car and made my way back to the hotel.

My next match was in a week. I needed to get my body back to as close to one hundred percent as I could, so that meant lots of vegetables and protein. I had to win this coming match. It was my only chance to get one step closer to my dream of getting out of Virginia Beach, because this sure as hell wasn't my dream. Virginia Beach was simply a stepping stone to bigger, better, and brighter things. I wanted the stage, and now that it was within sight, I could almost taste it.

I pulled my car into the parking spot in front of my room and cut the engine. Immediately, I noticed a car parked beside me. The trunk was open and filled with suitcases. The door next to my room stood wide open. *I must be getting a new neighbor,* I thought to myself as I climbed out and went around to my trunk. With my arms full, I made my way up to my door and was just about to put the key in the lock when I caught a glimpse of a woman. She darted out of the open door and made her way to the back of the car next to mine.

I glanced over at the pile of bags and boxes on the ground outside of the other door. She sure had a lot of stuff. That was one thing I had learned over the years: pack light. This couldn't be a weekender. *She must be an extended-stay*, I thought to myself.

I slipped the key into the lock and turned it, hearing the lock click open when I heard an agitated voice come from behind me.

"For fuck's sake, come on, get out of there, you stupid piece of crap!" I heard her groan and then start to swear.

I glanced over my shoulder, watching her reef on the bag she was trying to get out of her trunk. "You stupid piece of shit." She dropped the bag and stomped her foot on the ground and began trying to pull on the bag again.

I chuckled to myself, opened my door, and set my stuff down on the floor just inside the room. I closed my door, pocketed my keys, and walked around to the back of her car. I stood watching this tiny woman continue to struggle to get the last piece of luggage out of her trunk. She was an attractive girl—well, what I could see of her—and I was sort of enjoying watching her struggle for a second, until she dropped the bag again and wiped at her eyes.

"You need some help with that?" I asked, trying to come off as friendly as possible. I didn't want to startle her. I knew she had no idea I was behind her, and I knew most women were nervous around guys my size.

As soon as the words left my lips, she dropped the handle on the suitcase, her body tensed as the suitcase fell back into the trunk with a thud. She backed away from the car, spinning around to face me. The look of genuine fear on her face shocked me little at first, but then then I was the one who was shocked because of who stood in front of me.

"Katy?" I grinned. "What are you doing here?"

She didn't reply. Instead, she went pale, and the look of fear on her face almost sent me to my knees. "Are...Are...Have you been following me?" she murmured, backing away from me, holding her hands up in front of her, signaling for me to stay away as if I were going to hurt her.

I let out a laugh. "Not likely. I lived here first," I said, pointing to my glorious newfound home, and winked at her. I stepped forward as she took another step back from me. I held my hand out towards her to let her know I wasn't going to hurt her and reached into the trunk. I gripped the handle of her bag, and, in one swift motion, I pulled the first and then the second bag that were in the trunk. I smiled at her and carried them a few steps to the door of her room and set them inside the open door. Next thing I knew, she was standing beside me looking inside.

"You know, after all this, I'm beginning to think you may have a crush on me, that you've been following me perhaps," I teased, hoping to get a laugh out of her, but she didn't say anything. She just continued looking around the room, and then looked over to my door. She looked exasperated, stressed, and tired, and then those big blue eyes of hers met mine. They weren't as bright as they were the other night; they were actually very dark in color, as I really studied them, my eyes then falling to her lips. I could tell she was about to say something, so I waited, but as soon as she went to open her mouth, she burst into tears instead.

CHAPTER 10

Katy

I HAD HELD onto everything for so long that in one swift moment, without any control over myself, the tears just started to pour. Sobs literally shook my body as I buried my face in my hands. I could hear Jonas' words in the back of my mind. He was screaming at me to stop the fucking crying. Only weak people cry. Within seconds of remembering those harsh words, I got a grip on myself and wiped my eyes, and it was almost as if they had never started.

I looked up through blurry tear-filled eyes at Derrick. He stood there watching me, looking uncomfortable as if maybe he should run the other way. I wouldn't blame him if he did; it would be better for him in the long run.

I had been so determined to hate him because I thought he was exactly like Jonas. Only, in less than five minutes, I could already see that he wasn't anything like him. Jonas had never and would never voluntarily help me with anything. He got off making me ask, making me beg instead, before he would even lift a finger. He always wanted to remind me who was in charge and that every single second of every single day I needed him, would always need him, and that without him I was nothing. I'm sure that the reason I broke down was because Derrick had shown me kindness, not because I was afraid of him.

I blinked, and he stood there looking at me. I could tell he was trying to figure out how to handle me. I was a blubbering mess, and he had just paused for a moment and given me time to gather myself. He really should have just left me there because I wasn't even sure how to handle me or calm myself at this point, but he surprised me. Instead of running, he placed his large, warm hands on my shoulders and placed his finger under my chin, gently forcing my head up so I could look him in the eyes.

"I will be right back. Why don't you go inside and sit down in the chair." When I didn't move, he slowly guided me over to the chair in my room, one large hand on my shoulder, the other resting on my waist. I sat down, pulling my legs up underneath me. He went into my bathroom and came back carrying the toilet paper roll and handed it to me. "Sorry, there was no tissues." He shrugged. "I'll be right back."

He left the door to what was to be my new home wide open, which suddenly made me feel very vulnerable. What if Jonas was out there, lurking, just waiting for his chance to strike and get me? I had just about worked myself up into another panic attack when Derrick came back in through the door and handed me a bottle of water.

"I'm sorry, I don't have...anything. This isn't even cold. I just bought the case of water." He sighed, sitting down across from me, cracking the seal on his bottle and taking a sip without taking his eyes from me. He looked almost as if he had let me down, but he hadn't. He had shown me more kindness and support in the last five minutes than Jonas had shown me in the last five years.

I sucked in a deep breath, trying to calm myself. It was almost a struggle to even speak. "Thank you," I whispered, opening the bottle and taking a sip. "How are you feeling?" I asked, putting the cap back on the bottle.

"All right, I guess. Still badly bruised in the kidney area." He shrugged. He moved from where he was sitting on the end of the bed to the floor down in front of me. He crossed his legs and looked up at me.

I leaned forward and brushed my fingers over his eyebrow where the stitches should have been. "The stitches, they're gone. They should still be in there. Did you remove them yourself?"

He nodded. "I did." He grew quiet and sat there staring up at me. "What did I do earlier that upset you so?"

He frowned, trying to figure me out. "Or...is it not me at all?"

I licked my lips and wiped the tears from my eyes. I took a minute to think, trying to figure out how to tell him. This was going to be hard to share, since my co-workers didn't even know. I was so ashamed with myself at letting something like this go on that it had become an embarrassment. I dealt with young girls like this a million times in the hospital, and I always told them it was nothing to be embarrassed about. I would always assure them that it wasn't their fault either, but that was long before I knew what it felt like to be on the other side of the fence, and then I realized that what I told them was far easier said than done.

I swallowed hard, since I hadn't shared my situation with anyone except my close friends and that doctor I had worked for. It was hard to find the words. I wouldn't have shared it with the doctor if he hadn't guessed.

As I sat there looking at Derrick, I really had no idea how to even begin to tell him. He was basically a stranger to me, and I really wanted to maintain my pride. The longer he sat there looking into my eyes, the weaker I became. I needed someone in my life. I had been on my own long enough. However, the longer the words played back in my mind, the more I became afraid that he would leave. People always seemed to leave once they found out, whether by choice or through no fault of their own. I let out a breath. I really didn't even know why I cared about what he thought, but for whatever reason, I did.

"I'm...I'm on the run." The words fell from my lips in an almost silent whisper, and so did a ton of weight from my body from just that little confession.

He smiled. "You don't look like the kind of girl who would run from the law."

I knew he was just trying to make me laugh and calm me down, but I remained serious.

"I wish it were that." I admitted, "Somehow, I think that would be easier. I'm on the run from my ex." I frowned, reaching for my purse that sat on the table beside me. I rooted through the bag. I had kept a picture of Jonas, not because I wanted to remember what he looked like, but because I figured I might need it for the police or something. "This guy, Jonas," I said, finally pulling the picture from my purse and holding it out for him to take.

He reached and took the picture from me, his rough fingers grazing mine. He looked down at the tiny photograph. "Well, I can honestly say it's not a wonder why you hated me on sight." He looked back down at the photo, studying it for a second time, closer this time, almost as if he were memorizing it. "Let me guess, roids, right?" He handed me back the picture, and I put it back in my wallet.

"Well, you figured it out before I did, and I'm a nurse." I muttered, "Makes me feel sort of foolish and stupid." I zipped my purse closed and sat back, taking another sip of the warm water, trying to let myself relax.

"Why does it make you feel foolish? These guys aren't always easy to spot."

"Because you would think with my training I would have picked up on it." I shrugged.

"Listen, it's human nature. We never want to see the bad in someone we care about, and addicts are awesome liars. Don't blame yourself." He sighed and got quiet for a moment as I studied his eyes.

"Sounds like you've got experience with that," I whispered.

He nodded and set the water bottle on the floor beside him, leaning back on his hands. "My brother, he eventually overdosed on heroin. We all knew he had gotten mixed up with some bad people, but he insisted he was fine, so we looked the other way. Unfortunately, he wasn't fine, and after he was gone, I carried a lot of guilt, until I basically watched my mother waste away due to the guilt she carried. I'm all that is left, and I refuse to let what happened affect me like that. There was nothing I could have said or done to save him." He shrugged. "So believe me when I say it's not your fault."

"Wow, Derrick, I'm sorry."

"Don't be. We grew up in a rough neighborhood, and things were handled differently. It could have been me, instead, had I chosen a different path. I just thank my stars every day that it wasn't, and I know now that his choices were not my fault."

I watched his expressions as he finished talking. "I am sorry, Derrick," I murmured. It was all I could get out. I meant it, losing someone was hard, especially a sibling. I had seen it throughout my short career. The pain never left.

"How long have you been on the run?" he asked, looking up at me, changing the subject.

"I left the Midwest a few weeks ago. I had to sneak out while he was at the gym. Friends of mine helped me pack everything up. When he returned to the house that morning, he went ballistic. I know my neighbor called the police on him, but after that, I know nothing of what happened. All I know is that if I hadn't left when I did, he would have eventually killed me."

"He hit you?" Derrick asked, getting a little agitated.

I slowly nodded, the tears beginning to fall again as I thought back to the last time it had happened. "The last time he hit me, he left me with two black eyes and some severely bruised ribs, which are still sore if I move the right way," I said shyly.

Derrick didn't say anything; he sat their contemplating something. I couldn't tell now if he was going to walk out the door or not. "Do you think he is after you now?"

I nodded, looking at Derrick through blurry tear-filled eyes again. "I thought I would be safe and that I had done everything right and covered my tracks enough. I opened up all new e-mail and online accounts so he wouldn't be able to track me. I opened a new bank account so he couldn't track my money. I even changed all my pins for my credit cards. I registered my car here. I don't know what else I could have done to disappear," I whispered. "I even went as far to change my name legally. Well, my last name anyways. I was told you could do that if you were trying to hide. I just don't know how he has found me."

CHAPTER 11

Dagger

I sat there on the floor of her room trying to digest everything that she had told me. It was a lot for me to take in. I never understood guys like him. Men who hit women were weak and they pissed me off because they gave guys like me a very, very bad name. Within those seconds that she had confided in me I could already feel the adrenaline pumping through my veins. Suddenly, I felt protective of her and had a strong need to keep her safe. I wanted to protect her from him, which probably stemmed from the fact that I hadn't been able to protect my brother. I couldn't think like that, though, because I hadn't really been given the chance to save him. I could definitely help Katy build a new life, though, and at least give her a fighting chance. I knew I could; I just needed a minute to think.

"Do you by chance have a Gmail account?" I asked. She looked at me and nodded slowly. "Did you ever give him access to it?" She closed her eyes tight and once again nodded slowly.

"He made me," she whispered. "He claimed he wanted to keep me safe."

"Did you do any research or send e-mails about moving here while you were logged into that Gmail account?"

Her eyes widened and she placed her hand over her stomach as if she were going to be sick. "Well, I did, but I used a private browser at the library." She sank back into her seat, looking defeated.

"Sometimes a private browser works, sometimes not. Everything usually stays part of your google account history." I sighed.

"My God, what am I going to do?" she asked, her voice shaking. "I'm the one who led him straight to me. How stupid could I be?"

I could see the well of tears rimming her eyes, and I placed my hand on her knee. "First, you aren't stupid. Now, let's not panic. Let's log into your old account and take a look. I'll show you. We will see what we have and see if maybe we can't plant a seed to send him in another direction, that way it will bide you some time and you won't have to leave. Then we'll get you a new e-mail."

"Okay," she whispered, getting up from her seat and crossing the room.

My eyes followed her. She was an attractive girl and I couldn't help but check out her ass in her tight jeans as she grabbed a blue bag and brought it back over to where we were sitting. She smiled at me as she pulled the laptop from the bag. It was wrong in this situation to feel hopeful, but I wanted to get to know her better and, deep down in my gut, I didn't want her to have to go, which was terribly mean and selfish in light of the situation. I would do anything and everything I could to help her, even though she had made it clear the other night that she wanted nothing to do with me.

She waited for the laptop to boot up and then began typing away. I just hoped that she would follow my directions.

"All right, are you logged in?"

"Yep."

"Okay, do you see something that says 'my activity page?'" She nodded. "Click on it."

Her eyes widened as she looked at things on the screen. I got up on my knees beside her and rested my forearm on the arm of the chair. I pointed to the screen. "This tells him everything—pages you've visited, your location, things you've searched, even the ads you may have clicked on."

She sat there staring at the screen in front of her. "I can't believe it. I really am stupid," she murmured.

I ignored what she had said. It wasn't her. Most people knew nothing about this because, if they did, they would be much more careful about the things that they did online.

"Now if he knows how to get into the deeper information he will even have your calendar, contacts, and apps that are not only on your computer but on your phone as well."

"My God, Derrick, you're telling me that by giving him access to one simple thing, I have given him access to my entire life? I'm the one who brought him right to me?"

"It's possible. Is he computer savvy?" I hated to tell her the truth, but she needed to know.

She nodded, looking back down at the screen. "How do you know all this stuff anyways?" she asked quietly and glanced in my direction, meeting my eyes.

"I had a crazy ex," I admitted with a laugh. "She would make a point to show me if I had looked up an old female friend on Facebook." I could see a look in her eye that showed she was thinking ill thoughts of me again. "It's not what you think," I admitted.

"Really?" she said, eying me. I could tell she was having trouble believing me.

I shook my head. "Her name was Erika, my crazy ex. After my brother died, I wanted to reach out to Carly, the girl he had been dating all through high school but had recently broken up due to his changing behavior. I reached out to her to let her know personally that he had passed away. I didn't think it was right for her to find out any other way. I didn't know how to find her, so I searched for her online. Little did I know, Erika had been keeping tabs on me.

"She confronted me one night when I had gotten back from the gym, accusing me of cheating on her. I ended it with her shortly after that. For the longest time after I had moved out she was always messaging me with little clues that she knew where I was. She would make a comment about a coffee shop I had been at that morning, or comment on the fact that I had found a new health food store, and one night she asked me how the jeans fit from Calvin Klein, and that was when I realized that this was how she was still tracking me."

"So how did you fix it?"

"I deleted my old account and opened a new one. Then I moved."

"She was what made you come all the way out here?" she asked.

"Yes, aside from getting away from my psycho ex, my mother had remarried and was happily living with husband number five. They had no room for me in their lives. So since I had no one back home, and they had made it clear they had no room for me, I came here. Plus, the beach sounded really nice after growing up in a land-locked Midwest."

Katy gave me a soft smile. God, she was beautiful. "All right, show me where to find this," she said, pointing to the screen.

I helped her navigate the settings, and soon we were

sitting with one hell of a page of information. Everything she had done, everything she had searched about coming here from before she had left, sat right in front of us. We had everywhere she had stayed along the way, everywhere she had visited, apartments she had looked at, grocery stores she'd shopped at, places of employment she had applied to, everything was there. At one point, I glanced over at her and thought for a second that I saw her start to shake at what she was seeing. I rubbed my hand over her back, trying to comfort her.

"Okay, so planting false information. Is that step one?" she asked, taking a deep breath.

I nodded. "We can start with that. Once we have built up enough, we will stop using this account and set you up with a new one. However, I'm not sure you are going to like step two."

She inhaled deeply again. "What is step two?" she asked, her voice full of hesitation.

"We trade in your car and we get you something that he won't recognize," I said, looking into her eyes. She didn't need to be told how serious this was; she already knew.

"Okay."

"You'll have to lie low. You probably will have to change hotels eventually." I swallowed. "Just in case he has found you and doesn't follow the seeds we are going to plant." As soon as those words left my lips, something inside of me didn't like the thought of her going off alone. I didn't want her to be out of my sight, even for a split second, until I knew she was completely safe, that he was gone, and this was all over.

She took another deep, gulping breath. I'm sure she was thinking all of this over. She looked a little pale to me. "I...I don't suppose you would want to do this with me? Help me?"

I looked up at her. I could see the fear and uncertainty in her eyes, but I didn't know how to answer her.

"Truth is, Derrick, I could really use a friend. I've been so alone with no one to turn to, and to be honest, I would feel so much better having a bodyguard. I could...I could hire you?" she whispered.

Without even considering what all this might entail, I simply nodded. If it meant she was going to stay, then I would do it.

CHAPTER 12

Katy

We had talked in depth for a while about how I should cover my tracks, and I still sat there staring at the computer screen not knowing where to even start. All that kept running through my mind was that I had asked Derrick to protect me. Now I could barely even look at him. Those words had flown out of my mouth before I even thought about what him helping me actually meant. They had slipped out so fast that I really hadn't had a chance to stop them. This was how I had always gotten myself into trouble over the years. Up to and including now, this seemed to be a problem I had had my entire life, and I still hadn't learned my lesson: to actually think before I spoke. I had a pretty sweet thing going on right now. I forgot how great it was to be single. I could do whatever I wanted, with no one to answer to, and here I was going to complicate that.

I let out a deep sigh as I stared at that flashing cursor. I needed to stop. I wasn't getting into a relationship with Derrick. This was an agreement, a work arrangement. Nothing more. I knew that I needed Derrick, and I felt that I could trust him. I just had no idea how I would pay him. Between my car payment, rent, and food, there wasn't much leftover at the end of each month. Then it dawned on me: the money I received every month from the renters who were staying in my home. That money had been going into a savings account. Sarah normally deposited it into that account at the end of every month. I could use that money. I could transfer it to Derrick then, if he was willing to wait for it.

"Katy, what is it?" he asked, looking up from his phone and pulling me back to the moment.

I swallowed hard. I was so afraid of mucking things up with Derrick, just like I had done with Jonas. However, I also didn't want to die, so I needed to be upfront with him. People would think I was being a little overdramatic, but I wasn't. I knew what Jonas was capable of, I had seen it, and instantly my mind flashed back to a night last summer.

We were out at a bar. I had come out of the bathroom, and this guy had asked me if I had seen his girlfriend in the washroom. He had spoken to me, asked me a question, nothing more, but that was all it had taken. Jonas came up behind him, grabbed him by the neck, and threw him face first into the wall, breaking his nose—all because he had asked me a question. Pretty threatening. The man didn't deserve to be assaulted for that. I could only imagine what he would do if he found me here in a locked room with Derrick.

Now, as I sat here with him in front of me, I felt absolutely awful for even asking him to help me. I was afraid for Derrick. Jonas had warned me so many times that we were forever, and that we were meant to be, that I belonged to him. He always told me that nothing and no one would come between us. Instead, his mood swings and attitude came between us, and because of the way he treated me, that was what absolutely wrecked us.

I sat there pretending to read the screen in front of me, still ignoring the fact that Derrick had asked me a question. I was remembering all those sleepless nights I had spent with Jonas. Every fight we ever had ended with me curled up into myself in the far corner of our bed—a bed I was forced to sleep in, whether I wanted to or not. I would curl myself up so he couldn't touch me, and I would silently cry myself to sleep. I hurt, and I didn't know any other way to get it out of my system. He hated me when I cried and he would demand I stop every time.

"Katy, what is it?" Derrick asked again, bringing me back to the present.

"It's nothing," I murmured. "So what do we do?"

"Okay, so I think what we'll do is make up a life for you," Derrick said.

"We?" I tried to tell myself that this wasn't the same thing as what I had with Jonas; it wasn't even close. The man who sat before me had my best interests at heart. There was no way we could have any confusion between us either, no confusion on where we stood with one another; that was why I was paying him. I had drawn our line in the sand, and neither of us could cross it. That meant I was safe, and I wouldn't end up where I had before. Within those few moments, the way I looked at Derrick changed. I was looking at him like he was an old, trusted friend instead of a threat, and I sat there listening and hanging onto every word he spoke.

"Log into the hotel Wi-Fi," he said, standing up and sitting on the arm of the chair beside me.

I did as I was told, trying to ignore the comforting warmth that radiated from his body. As he leaned in closer to me to see the screen, I couldn't help but catch the scent of his cologne. I cleared my throat and took a sip of the water Derrick had brought me. "Now what?" I asked.

"All right, first, we are going to need a list of places. It would be better if we make it look frantic, like you're seriously trying to figure out what your next steps might be." He pulled his phone from his pocket and pulled up a map of the surrounding areas.

I typed in a few of the cities he suggested, going to their city sites and flipping through the pages of each one, spending enough time on each page to make it look like I was reading it.

"Maybe look for a few jobs too, even apply to some. We want to make it look as believable as we can. Also, we should apartment hunt," he urged as he sat beside me, continuing to look over my shoulder.

"Yeah, but how believable?" I asked as I nibbled on my bottom lip.

"As believable as we can. He isn't going to be able to tell if you actually go through with anything. He will just be able to see where you were. That's it. We want to lead him away from here, make him think that you just stopped here, and that you are on your way out of town," he said, blowing out a breath.

I continued searching the city's websites, finally choosing one about forty miles north. Then I went to job sites that were located in that area. I did as suggested and even applied to a couple medical jobs, putting down the last hotel's phone number and address on the applications. Then I pulled up some apartment listings and filled out the applications. We spent the better part of the afternoon creating false tracks that hopefully Jonas would follow.

"That's great. This looks good," Derrick said, nodding at all the work I had done. "Oh, and also while I am thinking of it, if I am going to look out for you, then we should probably accept one another on the 'Find my Friend' app as well. That way I can keep an eye on you when you aren't with me," he said, picking up his phone and waiting for my information.

In that instant, fear built up inside of me. Jonas had kept watch on me that way as well. I hesitated reaching for my phone.

"What is it, Katy?" he asked, waiting.

"It's just, Jonas used to keep track of me in a similar way. I'd stop off somewhere after work, and when I would get home, he would question me as to why I had stopped."

"Well, there is a difference: I'm not doing it for controlling reasons. I'm doing it to make sure I know where you are and that you are safe. You can do whatever you want, go wherever you want, you'll never hear it from me. It's just more for my peace of mind when I am not with you, and you will know where I am and how far I am from you should you need me. Does he still track you that way?"

"He might. I never thought of changing that account," I murmured.

"Do you know how he did it."

"He said something about a tracker."

"Give me your phone."

I placed my phone in his hand and watched as he searched through it, finally finding what he was looking for.

"Found it and disabled it." He smiled. I felt bad questioning him about this, but his answer made sense. "All right, now let's get you set up on Friend Finder."

He went about setting everything up and handed me

my phone. He quickly showed me how to use it. Somehow, knowing he would know where I was when I wasn't
with him made me feel better. It made me feel at ease
knowing where he was at all times, and this would help
him look out for me when I was at the hospital as well.

"Are you hungry?"

I nodded, sipping on my water. "I haven't eaten much
today. I was in such a rush to get away from my other
place."

"Give me a minute." He got up off the floor and went
back to his room, returning with a vegetable tray for us to
snack on while we continued creating more of a frantic
plan. By the time eight rolled around, we had left a lot of
tracks and breadcrumbs for Jonas to follow. I just prayed
that it worked.

A few hours later, we sat cross-legged on the floor,
veggie tray between us. "Do you think we have done
enough?" I asked, glancing at the time and seeing it was
now dark outside.

"I think it's a very good start," he answered, crunching
on a carrot. "Now for the car," he gently reminded me.

I shut the laptop down and rubbed my eyes. I had
been struggling with that part of the plan all day. I
should've been smarter. I should've dumped the car first
thing. Instead, I had been too busy running. I had been an
idiot. The car was one of the only things I still had from
my old life, and I think that was why I was having such a
hard time. The car...had been purchased before Jonas and

was basically all I had left of the real me before all of this happened.

"I have no idea what to buy. I have...money and credit. It's not that..." I said, starting to panic.

"Whoa...Whoa...it's okay." He held his hand out for me to take. "We'll go in the morning. We will ride in your vehicle together. I will help you pick a new car. It will be awesome, you'll see."

He seemed determined to make this fun and exciting, and I tried hard to let go of how painful it was for me to give up everything, all because someone who wasn't worth another breath from my life was terrorizing me. While I watched him to try to make light of this for me, I tried my hardest not to wonder what Derrick would be like as a boyfriend, because as a bodyguard and a friend, he was pretty freaking awesome.

CHAPTER 13

Dagger

AFTER THE GYM the next morning, I ran home and showered, then I went next door. It was only eight, but I figured
Katy would already be up. Instead of knocking, I sent a
quick text and was surprised when not two seconds later a
text was waiting for me. I waited outside for her to open
the door.

"Morning," she said, taking a seat down on the floor in
front of her computer.

I looked around the room. The curtains were shut
tightly, the dresser had been moved from where it had
originally sat, closer to the door, and Katy looked
exhausted.

"You ready to go?" She looked up at me with very tired blue eyes and a soft smile.

"Just give me one minute."

"Sure," I said, sitting down on the edge of the bed and waiting. As I looked around the room, I wondered if she had actually slept. The bed was still made, her bags still packed, and she wore the same clothes she had on yesterday.

"Did you move the dresser?" I asked.

She looked up at me and nodded. "I blocked the door, that way if he came, I would have time to hide." She hid her eyes from me the second the declaration was out. I said nothing. I felt bad for her and didn't want her to be ashamed.

A few minutes later, she closed her laptop down. "I'm ready." She held out her hand for me to take.

I pulled her up off the floor and walked over to the door while she slipped her shoes on. I opened the door and stepped outside and looked over my shoulder to see her trudging along behind me. She needed to do this, and my plan was to make this as easy and painless as possible for her. I could tell she didn't want to get rid of her car, but at this point, I also knew that she didn't have a choice.

She threw me the car keys and I caught them just before they hit the ground. "Oh no, Katy, you are driving," I said, holding them out for her to take.

"No, it's okay. You probably wouldn't want to drive with me anyways."

I looked at her. Probably another line of shit that asshole had spewed to her. "Take the keys, come on," I said, still holding them out toward her. I wanted her to feel calm and as confident as possible. She needed to build up and keep those traits about her. I wasn't giving her any other choice, so I hopped into the passenger seat. She looked at me through the windshield and then trudged around to the driver's side and climbed in.

"All right, where are we going? I don't know the area all that well," she said as she fired up the engine and placed her purse on the floor by my feet, her arm grazing my leg.

"I think we'll head to CarMax," I said, checking the mirror as she put the car in reverse and backed out. "Do you know how to get there?" She shook her head. "No worries, it's not very far from here."

I had purchased every single vehicle I had owned from them. They made buying a vehicle easiest. There was no haggling, which made me happy. She was in absolutely no condition to haggle anyways. She was barely holding it together as it was; I could see it in her eyes, in everything she did, and every word she said, and I barely knew her. The girl who sat beside me right now was a far cry from the girl I had met only a week or so ago in the emergency room.

"Okay, so before we get there, we should at least decide what you want. Did you want another car or would you like a minivan or SUV instead?" I asked her while we were stopped at a stoplight. I wanted her to be less over-whelmed when we got there, instead of walking in and dumping everything on her all at once. I didn't want some pushy salesman pushing her into something she didn't want, either, just because she couldn't make up her mind.

She looked out the window at two people walking down the street, and then glanced to me, her eyes taking on a bit of laughter. "A truck, complete with a bully bar." She let out this cute little giggle. "I'm joking, for the most part. Jonas used to have a truck with a bully bar," she said, getting serious again.

I nodded, smiling. I was about to tell her that they weren't very practical when I realized she had been joking.

"I think we should look at SUVs. I don't want anything that makes me feel like I am driving a bus, but perhaps a vehicle big enough to, say, transport a body, rugged enough to dump it in the woods, but cute enough that no one would ever suspect me." She winked, finally giving me a small smile.

I couldn't help but grin. She was way too cute when she was trying to be tough. "Hate to break it to you, sweetie, but if you were going to kill him, you probably wouldn't have moved and we wouldn't be having this conversation right now. I don't want you to be scared, but I like that you are thinking defensively."

"I'm trying." She smiled and let out a breath.

"I want you to be strong and assertive, like you were with me that night in the ER."

"Yeah, about that." She hesitated, tapping her thumb on the steering wheel. "I'm sorry."

I shook my head before she could say anything else. "No worries. The way you failed to succumb to my charms makes a lot more sense now. No wonder you had a natural hatred toward me."

"I didn't hate you. I just...didn't trust you." Katy shrugged and looked at me apologetically.

"It's all right. Don't feel bad. I'm tough, even though you secretly crushed my heart. I just hope you can trust me now." I winked back.

"I think I can."

As I looked at her, I had a feeling that I would never be able to stay mad at her. I shook my head. It was taking everything I had to keep my hands to myself. Every time I looked over at those eyes and those pouty, full lips, all I wanted to do was take her in my arms, kiss her, and make everything okay. Sadly, though, it wasn't as easy as that. I would have been happy just to hold her hand even. The second she had finished telling me everything yesterday, I'd wanted to hold her and never let her go. She was special, and she deserved so much more than the life she had gotten and was continuing to get.

As she drove and I sat there watching her, I already knew I wanted to be the one to see to it that she got everything that she deserved and more. She deserved to have every shot that she wanted to take and have all the support in doing those things. That was what good guys did for their dream girls. Instead, she had been stuck with this dick, who didn't deserve anything, especially her. Unfortunately, I knew where I stood; I was now the hired help, nothing more, and I wondered if she didn't do that to keep us apart. I looked over at her. She was beautiful as she concentrated on the road in front of her.

"What?" she asked as she stopped at another light.

"Nothing." I knew from the way she looked at me in that second that my chances with her had been ruined before I had even met her. She had been hurt by one of my own kind, and the quicker I let go of any hope and dream I had of having her, the better off I would be.

I could see the sign for CarMax approaching on the left, and I pointed it out to her to give her time to get in the right lane. I could see the worry etched on her face as she pulled into the parking lot and into the first empty parking spot, shutting the engine off.

"You have nothing to worry about. I will back you up in there, but this is your thing okay? You are the one in charge; you are the one who says what goes. You don't like something, you say so." I could see her starting to doubt herself already. This guy had really done a number on her. "If you need help, ask me anything you want, tell me what it is you need, but I know you can do this," I encouraged.

She took a deep breath, her hands holding tight to the steering wheel. I could see she was trying to work up the nerve to make this happen.

"What are you thinking?" I asked quietly.

"I just never used to question my abilities. Now I question them in everything I do, except work," she muttered. "Not before Jonas anyways. If I wanted something, I would go out and get it. I used to think I could do anything I put my mind to. Now, I automatically think everything I do is going to fail. It's a challenge."

I reached out and placed my hand on her thigh. Her eyes followed to where my hand sat and back up to my eyes, and I quickly pulled my hand away. "You still can, Katy. You can do anything you put your mind to. Just look at yourself."

"Look at what? I'm a neurotic mess who can't sleep unless I barricade my door with a dresser, for God's sake, and even then I sometimes can't."

"I don't think so. You moved across the country, you found a new place to live, you applied and were hired at a new job." I grinned, trying hard to build her up. "Neurotic messes don't do those things."

"So what does all that prove? That I am coward that couldn't tell my boyfriend to get out."

"It proves that you're smart enough to see the difference between doing something stupid and dangerous. You're amazing. You took control of a situation you no longer wanted to be in and got out. You know, most women would have stayed. Most women wouldn't have even recognized the trouble they were in. Give yourself a little bit of credit. Now hold your head up and let's go buy you a new vehicle." I squeezed her shoulder and looked into her eyes.

She smiled up at me. Like, truly smiled. It was like no one had ever spoken to her like that before. That smile made my cheeks turn crimson and my ears burn.

"Thank you, Derrick," she whispered, placing her hand over mine. She surprised me by leaning over and kissing my cheek. "No matter what happens from now on, thank you." She grabbed her purse and hopped out of the car, shutting the door without another look back.

I sat there feeling bad because that sweet, soft kiss meant as a thank you to a good friend went straight to my cock, and heat began coursing through my body. I climbed out of the car, the cool air hitting my hot face, and walked over to see what Katy was looking at. I kept my eyes on the car, not her ass, as she bent to look inside one of the other vehicles. I'll admit, I was happy for the distraction because, no sooner had we started looking at the car, we were approached by one of the sales guys.

"Can I help you?" he asked.

I cleared my throat. "We are here looking for a vehicle for my friend," I answered, turning things over to Katy, while I backed off and stood on the sidelines.

CHAPTER 14

Katy

Two hours later, we were sitting in the office inside of CarMax. John, the sales guy, had gone to make copies of the paperwork. I sat there chewing my nails. I was still nervous, afraid I had made some sort of huge mistake. I fiddled with the few flyers that sat on John's desk, picking each one up and looking at it, when I felt Derrick's hand squeeze my shoulder. I knew he had been in the room standing behind me, leaning against the wall the entire time in case I needed him.

"Relax, you're doing great. I think you are going to be very happy with this vehicle," he whispered in my ear, his warm breath grazing my cheek. "To be honest, it was a steal." He squeezed both of my shoulders in his strong hands, releasing some of the tension I was holding. "The best part is that once you actually realize it's all yours, and that it was purchased on your own, and picked by you, nothing can ever take the joy of this away from you."

He was right. We sat there in the quiet room, and I slowly relaxed back into the seat, his hands still resting on my shoulders, the warmth of him sinking into me as he continued gently massaging them. As I relaxed under his touch, I realized that Derrick really was the polar opposite of Jonas. Instead of taking things from me, he was pushing me forth into the world. The difference was that he stood beside me, giving me all the confidence and little pushes I needed to make the decisions I had faced today. He had even answered all of my questions, never once making me feel stupid for asking.

As soon as John flew back into the room, Derrick ripped his hands away from my shoulders, and I instantly felt the void. John set the papers in front of me and handed me a pen, and there I signed over my first car in exchange for a very nice black SUV.

I felt like I was on top of the world as I stepped out of CarMax with the keys. It wasn't much of a big deal to some, I know—people do this every day—but for me it was a huge deal. It was such a little thing, but I felt as if it had given me back some of my independence. I was beginning to prove to myself that perhaps I could take my life back. I had handed so many little pieces of myself over to Jonas on a silver platter, every time I did what he wanted, which had destroyed every last inch of me. It was going to take some time to get it back.

Before one of the lot guys took my old car away, we quickly took my belongings from my old car and transferred them to the new one. Once we were done and seated in the new car, Derrick placed his hand on mine.

"Do you have that picture of him again?" Derrick asked. "I want make sure I have his face committed to memory."

I studied his face and then reached down into my purse. I would have just sent him one through social media, but after I had learned all I had this afternoon, I had closed down my Facebook account completely, which was the only other place I had pictures of him. I pulled out my wallet, found the photo, and held it while Derrick took a picture of it.

"Great, thanks," he whispered.

I don't know why I was expecting a reaction from him, maybe some acknowledgment of what an asshole Jonas was, but he said nothing. He took the picture and shoved his phone back in his pocket.

We drove back to the motel in silence. I pulled into my parking spot and sat there as Derrick went to pull on the handle to open the door. I chewed my bottom lip, looking straight ahead. I had another question to ask Derrick, but for some reason, I was almost afraid to ask.

"What's on that mind of yours?" he asked, clearing his throat.

"How do you know something is on my mind?" I questioned.

"You get quiet and chew your bottom lip," he answered, smiling.

"When should we move?" I asked quietly.

He let out a breath. "Well, I just moved here a week ago, and you yesterday. I guess we could look into some new places in time. We should do a search first, though, and then we'll have to scope them out. Maybe I could do that while you're working at the hospital this week."

"Okay."

"No worries, we are only going to move if we have to." He frowned, taking in my worried gaze. "Obviously, you are off tonight?"

"I am. I work three days on, two off, alternating between days and nights. It's a rotating schedule because I work ten-hour shifts." I shrugged. "It's not that bad. I'm getting used to it, but I hate the overnights. I never know who may come in through those doors on a night shift, and I always fear he may sneak into the hospital that way. You know, when it's quiet and there is less security."

"I hear you. Well, I am paid up until the end of the week, so if we need to move, that should give me plenty of time to scope out a new place."

That answer satisfied me, and I climbed out of the car and went inside. Derrick followed me into my room and sat on the edge of the bed, while I sat down in the uncomfortable chair. I was still chewing my bottom lip, a look of worry surely seated on my face.

"What is it, Katy?" he asked, squatting down in front of me and resting his hands on my thighs. Something about his touch felt so comfortable and safe.

"What about tonight?" I bit my lower lip and waited. Ever since I had seen the handprint on the car window after my shift last night, I had been freaked out. I was constantly looking over my shoulder. I had pulled the dresser across the door and tried my hardest to sleep the night before, but with all the strange noises, I couldn't.

Derrick studied me for a moment. "Are you scared of being on your own?"

"A little. I have barely any food either. I haven't made the time to shop." I swallowed hard, biting my thumbnail.

"Did you want to stay with me in my room?"

I knew he was watching me for a reaction. I looked around my room. My bags were still sitting inside the door, packed tightly. I had only paid for one night, because I was unsure whether I was staying in the area or not.

"Katy?"

"I only paid for one night. I didn't know if I would end up staying or not," I whispered.

"All right, well, if you want to stay with me, that is fine. That way it will save you the money."

I slowly nodded and shyly smiled. As if we were thinking the same thing, he said, "There is only one bed, though." Just as the words passed his lips, a car door slammed outside. Derrick was up and over to the window in seconds, parting the curtains to look outside.

I nodded again. "I know I hated you the other day, but I didn't know you yet," I mumbled, shying my face away from him.

"It's fine. We don't have to sleep together. I will get them to drop a roll-a-way into my room. It's probably just a small fee, and that way you can have the king-sized bed all to yourself." Without waiting any longer, he grabbed my suitcases and moved them out of my room and over to his. I grabbed the other few things I had and moved them to his room as well, doing one final check to make sure I had everything before dropping the key off at the main office.

DERRICK HAD GONE to pick us up dinner, while I unpacked a few things from my bigger bags: my toiletries, my pajamas and clothes for tomorrow morning. Once I was finished, I went and sat down on the bed and turned the TV on, quickly finding an episode of *Friends* to watch. Jonas never let me watch TV, or at least never anything I wanted to watch, unless of course he wasn't home.

I had just gotten settled when the door swung open, causing me to jump up. Derrick stood there with two bags from the grocery store. He smiled and stepped inside and placed the two bags on the counter of the little kitchenette.

"All right, I just went over to the hot table. Roasted

chicken and potatoes for you," he said, handing me a cardboard container, "and the same for me." He shut and locked the door, and then sat down and opened his container, taking a couple of bites. "Did you happen to remember to call for the roll-away while I was gone?"

I shook my head. "I'm sorry, I forgot," I mumbled, shying away from him. Truth was, I didn't really want him to sleep in a separate bed. After all, I was the one intruding on his space. If anything, it should be me. Besides, I just wanted a little human interaction. I had been alone for a while, and I desperately needed to feel someone next to me.

"Well, I should probably call then because, if not, they are apt not to have any. The parking lot was getting rather full when I came in." He got up and grabbed the phone receiver and began to dial.

I didn't wait. I placed my food on the bedside table and stood up, walking over behind him and placing my hand on his bicep. He turned and looked at my hand and then down into my eyes, the receiver slowly falling away from his ear until it was back on its cradle.

"I really need to be held. Do you think you could do that, just for tonight?" I could barely hear my own voice as the words fell from my lips, my heart pounding wildly in my chest.

Derrick stood there silent as he stared at me, no doubt trying to figure me out. Now I did sound like a neurotic mess. He opened his arms and wrapped them around me, pulling me against him. At first, I was scared as he closed his arms around me, and then a strange calmness settled over me. It was as if my body had exhaled, like a weight had been lifted off me, and for the first time in the past few months, I finally felt safe.

CHAPTER 15

Dagger

My HEART RATE accelerated as she wrapped her arms around me, her touch sending millions of shock waves through my body all at once. I stood in the middle of the room with my arms wrapped tightly around her, her cheek resting on my chest. She fit against me so perfectly—almost too perfectly, her hot little body pressed up against mine. The gentle puff of her breath as she relaxed into me dancing along my shirt, almost instantly I knew I was in trouble. *Just hold her all night.* Yeah, sure, I could do that, or I could totally screw everything up because I was much better at doing that.

I stood there quietly holding her, letting her rest against me. I couldn't believe how she was holding everything together. Most women would have crumbled. This just showed me how strong she really was, and that turned me on more than anything. I had no expectations about how this was going to work. She had been a pro at the dealership, not afraid to speak up when she needed or ask me questions when she felt she didn't know something. She was smart and strong the entire time. Now she was letting her guard down, and that was okay with me too; whatever she needed. She rested her head on my shoulder, her face buried into the crook of my neck, and inhaled deeply.

"Did you want to go for a drive?" I whispered. She nodded against my shoulder. Thank God she had said yes. I didn't know how much longer I could stand there holding her without trying to kiss her.

We drove around the city, talking and laughing, and an hour later, we were parked up by a private lake. I loved this place and always came here for some downtime, which I knew she needed badly. We sat in quiet, just looking out over the water, and she slowly slid her hand into mine. A light rain started to fall, and soon the windshield was covered, so I started up the engine.

"We should probably head back," I said, swallowing hard and rubbing her small hand that still sat in mine.

"Oh, all right, I suppose." She pulled her seatbelt on.

"I think I will drive by your old place on the way home. I want to see if you recognize any of the vehicles parked there." If the bastard was stalking her, he might not know that she had fled the place already.

"Okay." The tone of her voice told me that she was scared to do this. I turned on the radio and placed my hand on the centre of the seat, palm up, waiting for her to take it again. She did so without hesitation.

"It's okay, you're with me. I won't let anything happen to you," I said, rubbing my thumb over the back of her hand.

I pulled into the parking lot of her old building. "Okay, let me know if you recognize any of the cars okay?" I said, driving slowly through. She looked out the window and nodded. "So what makes you think he is following you?"

She was quiet for a minute, as she continually looked at all the cars in the parking lot. "There was a handprint on my window the other night after I finished work," she whispered.

I frowned, waiting for her to continue. Surely, she wasn't basing all of this off a single handprint. That could have been anyone.

"That used to be his...thing. He loved holding his hand up to mine to show me and remind me how tiny and insignificant I was, especially when he was pissed off with me. After a while, it was just to remind me how he could crush me like a bug." I could see tears in her eyes as she shook her head sadly. "I don't see any vehicle I recognize, Derrick," she mumbled.

"Okay, vehicles are irrelevant. What about people? Do

you see anyone that you recognize?" I asked, slowing down on what was now our third, perhaps fourth, drive-by. She shook her head as she watched out the window.

As I drove slowly through the parking lot, I glanced over at her. The look on her face was pure fear. The more I thought about the handprint that had been on her window, the more I believed her. She was really scared, and I knew she wasn't imagining things. She wasn't a girl who made things up. I needed to be on alert, and I felt adrenaline start to course through my veins. This guy was here somewhere, and I was going to make sure he didn't get to her.

Once we returned and I had parked my car, we walked together to the room, stopping to grab a coke from the vending machine. Once inside, we made short work of locking down my room, dead bolting and chaining the door and pulling the curtains together tightly. I wasn't worried about man-to-man competition. I would wipe the floor clean with him, but I was worried that he may bring a gun or knife to a fist fight. Still, I was serious and stoic and was determined to keep her safe. It had nothing to do with the little she was paying me either; we hadn't even talked numbers yet. At the moment, I didn't even care if I worked for free.

After everything was locked down, we turned the TV on and found something to watch. I grabbed the spare pillows from the closet and built them up behind us against the headboard. We relaxed back and started watching TV. With the curtains pulled, it was dark in the room, and soon she was letting out these little yawns, almost fighting to stay awake.

"Why don't you go get ready for bed," I suggested and nodded towards the bathroom. "Have a hot shower. Take as long as you'd like."

"You sure?" she questioned.

Did he not let her even relax in the shower, I wondered to myself.

"Yes, I'm sure. Go." I winked at her.

She nodded and hopped down from the bed and went to her bag. She reached in and pulled out some sleep clothes and her toiletries and made her way to washroom. As soon as the door clicked shut, I got up and made my way over to my stuff. I pulled my shirt off over my head and removed my jeans, exchanging them for sleep pants. I didn't normally sleep in anything, but I felt that perhaps a layer of something between us may not be a bad idea.

I grabbed the extra blanket from the closet, in case she got cold, and spread it over the bed. Then I adjusted my pillows against the headboard again and relaxed back on the bed watching TV. I lay there listening to the shower run, thinking thoughts that shouldn't have been running through my mind. What it would have been like to go and crawl into that shower behind her and kiss away every last worry she had. Make her feel worshiped like the woman she was supposed to be, and take away every last waking thought of that asshole.

Minutes later, the shower finally shut off, and I turned my thoughts back to the TV and blew out a breath, adjusting my already semi-hard cock. I can do this, I thought to myself. *We are only sharing a bed.* Five minutes later, the door to the bathroom clicked open and she emerged wearing a racer-back tank top and some booty shorts. I couldn't help my eyes running over her body as she placed her dirty clothes into another bag. Thank God she hadn't met my eyes. I wouldn't have been able to hide the thoughts running through my mind. I groaned to myself. I was definitely going to need more than a layer or two of blankets between us. Good thing I had grabbed the extra blanket from the closet because I had a feeling I would need that as well.

She walked over to her side of the bed, and I pulled back the covers so she could crawl in beside me, pulling them over top of her. Then I reached over and shut the light off and shuffled my body down so I was lying beside her, adjusting the blankets and relaxing. I flipped the TV to another show and turned the volume down. I placed both arms behind my head and relaxed, trying to stop all the thoughts running through my mind.

Five minutes into the show, Katy scooted over towards me and rested her head on my chest, her arm around my waist. She was just about relaxed when I felt her body stiffen.

"Is this okay?" she asked.

I rested my arm around her. I wanted her to know that

it was fine. I had no problems with her curling up against me, especially if it was what she needed at the moment, even if it was killing me.

"Sure. Did you want me to shut the TV off so you can get some rest?" I asked, reaching for the remote.

"Leave it on, just for the noise. I have a hard time sleeping," she answered quietly. So instead, I dimmed the brightness a little.

"It's okay, rest, I'm here." I shimmied and turned my body towards her and pulled her into me. She obviously needed to be held; I could tell. I wrapped both arms around her as she pushed her little body against mine as close as she could possibly get. I could feel myself growing hard and was thankful that some of the blankets were tucked between us. I didn't want her to think I wanted that from her.

As we lay there, her breath gently puffing against my skin, I felt a tiny kiss on my chest. I pulled back and looked down at her, her tired eyes meeting mine. She didn't shy away, like she normally did. Instead, she reached up and placed her tiny, warm hand on my cheek, while still looking into my eyes. She brought her lips to mine. It started out as only a light peck, but then she actually kissed me.

I pulled back and studied her eyes. Inside of them I saw a spark of something, a need, a want, but before this went any further, I needed to make sure it was what I thought it was, because this was exactly how I ended up fucking things up. She didn't wait for me to decide, though. Instead, she crashed into me, kissing me frantic and hard.

I rolled her over and propped myself up on my elbow, letting her body relax and lie against the mattress. My other hand rested on her waist while I met her lips, sweeping my tongue through her mouth. There was no need to rush. I was going to take my time with her. I didn't want to blow things with this girl, and I was afraid if we rushed, it might appear that that was all I wanted. I also wanted her to know that if she decided she wanted to stop, that would be okay too.

As I kissed her, I felt her hand trail down my side and stop, resting on my hip. As I continued to kiss her, I real- ized that I was almost afraid to touch her. She had been through a traumatic experience, and the last thing I wanted was to find myself in trouble with the law, so I decided I was just going to let her lead, and wherever that took me would be fine.

My kiss got a little deeper the longer this went on, my tongue sweeping through her mouth again and again. I was fully straining against my sleep pants, my cock throb- bing with the need to be inside her, and then she let out this little moan that pretty much shook me to my core. She was killing me.

She tilted her head to the side, and I took the opportu- nity to kiss and suck on the side of her gorgeous neck, careful not to leave any type of marks. She reached down to where my hand was still resting on her hip and took my hand in hers, lacing our fingers together.

"Touch me, Derrick," she whispered in my ear as I continued to kiss her neck. "Touch me, make me feel wanted."

At the sound of her plea, it was as if I had been struck by lightning. She let go of my hand, placing hers on the back of my neck. I pulled the covers from between us and reached down and gripped her ass, pulling her closer to me. I wanted her to feel exactly how wanted she was, how hard I was for her.

I allowed my hands to roam her body, gently brushing my thumb over her breast. I could feel her hardened nipple through her tank top. I felt her shimmy and lift her butt a little. I figured she was just getting comfortable, but as my hand ran down to cup her ass again, I realized she wasn't wearing those cute fucking booty shorts anymore. She had slipped them off, and I let out a throaty groan as my cock continued to throb. That was when I felt her hand reach into the back of my sleep pants, gripping my ass.

I continued kissing her mouth, wishing she would touch me but trying my hardest not to let her know that. This all had to be on her terms. I sucked her bottom lip into my mouth, and that was when her tiny hand finally found my cock. She took me in her hand, lightly gripping me, and ran her fingers over me. The moment that I felt those soft hands run over me, I knew I was in trouble. She began pushing at the waistband of my pants, and I obliged her by kicking them off.

Continuing to kiss her and run my tongue through her mouth, she dropped my cock and gripped my hand, lacing our fingers together again. Our kissing soon slowed to a comfortable pace, and then she yet again shocked the shit out of me. Taking my hand and placing it between her legs, this time I couldn't help but moan a little. She was completely bare and I could feel her hot, wet heat. I pulled away from her and looked down into her eyes. No words needed to pass between us. From the dim light of the TV, I could already see it in her eyes: she wanted this, she wanted me.

I leaned down, placing my lips on hers, and then I softly ran my fingers through her wetness and over her clit. She kissed me harder, as soon as they ran over her clit again. She was extremely wet, and the less pressure I put on her clit, the more responsive she was. She gripped my cock, jerking it and gripping it a little harder now, running her thumb through the bead of precum that sat waiting for her.

"Come here." I moaned as I took her hand off my cock. I gripped her ass and rolled onto my back, pulling her with me so she was now straddling my waist. I could feel her heat pouring onto me as she sat up and pulled her top off, exposing her perfect, full breasts to me. I was hesitant at first, but then reached up and ran both my hands over them, taking a moment to roll her nipples between my thumb and fingers. I felt her body shudder, and she dropped her head back, exposing her neck to me. I quickly sat up and kissed that little spot on her collarbone.

I wrapped my arms around her, pulling her body closer to me. I could feel her wetness on my cock and knew that if we moved a certain way I would have perfect access to slide into her.

"Do you have protection?" I heard her whisper in my ear as she sucked my lobe into her mouth, causing a shudder to roll through my body.

Holding her close to me, I reached into the bedside drawer and fumbled around for the open box of condoms. I quickly tore the package open and handed her the condom. I lay back, putting my arms behind my head, and watched the expression on her face as she looked from me to the condom.

"Go ahead," I whispered and ran my hand through her hair, resting it on her cheek.

She gripped my cock in her hand and pumped it a couple of times—not that it needed it—and then she rolled the condom over me. I loved watching the shy look on her face. She was so beautiful, her cheeks holding a hint of pink.

She straddled my waist again and placed my hands down to rest on her waist while she slid my cock through her wetness. She lined me up and took her time, allowing me to slide into her. I watched her face, her head dropping back, her eyes closing, the look of pure pleasure written on her face, while my cock slowly slid into her. I wanted to keep watching her but couldn't. She felt so damn good, hot, wet, and fucking tight. Once I was buried deep inside of her, she bent down and met my lips, letting out a throaty moan as I started to move inside of her.

I gripped her hips with my hands, guiding her movement. Pushing myself deeper into her. Sitting up, I wrapped my arms around her, pulling her into me while she continued to ride me. She held onto me, moaning into my ear as she began to tighten around me. She moaned into my neck, and I felt the rush of heat from her as she gripped my shoulders tighter.

In one swift movement, I lay down with her wrapped in my arms and quickly spun us so I was now on top of her. Her knees rested on either side of my hips and I began to thrust into her, deeper, harder, and faster. Her breath matched my movement, and I felt her tighten around me again, only this time, I came with her, hard and fast.

As I came down, I looked down at her as she lay beneath me. She looked up at me, a calm, safe look in her eyes, and I leaned down and placed a soft kiss on her lips.

"Give me a minute," she whispered into my mouth.

I rolled off her and watched as she got up and wandered into the bathroom. I quickly cleaned myself up, tying and throwing the condom in the garbage, and crawled back into bed. I relaxed back, placing my hands behind my head, waiting for her to return. The longer she was gone, the more afraid I was that this had all been a mistake. I certainly didn't feel that way, but I was afraid she might.

I was just about to call out to her when the bathroom door opened and the light went out. She didn't make eye contact with me; she just walked over and crawled into bed, pulling the covers over her, and slid over up against my body. As badly as I wanted to ask her if she was okay, I didn't question anything. I just relaxed, placed my arm under her neck, and wrapped the other around her waist, pulling her tightly against me. She was asleep within minutes, and soon her deep, steady breathing lulled me to sleep.

CHAPTER 16

Katy

I WOKE WITH A START, my heart pounding in my chest, my body hot and sweaty. I opened my eyes, blinking hard. The room was still dark, and I was having a hard time trying to figure out where I was at first, and then I felt the bed move.

It didn't take me long to remember when I felt the comforting warmth of Derrick's body pressed up against mine. His arm was slung around my waist, his other arm still under my neck, holding me. I started to calm instantly as I placed my hand on top of his and he laced his fingers with mine.

I lay back down and pulled the covers up over my cold, bare shoulder and relaxed again. I felt so safe and comfortable in his arms and wanted to stay like that forever. I was just about asleep again when I felt the bed move again, only this time Derrick's warmth left me.

"Derrick?" I murmured in an almost sleep state.

"It's okay, it's okay, go back to sleep. I'm just going to hit the gym," he said, pulling the blanket down a bit to kiss my bare shoulder before heading to the bathroom to shower.

I drifted in and out of sleep, and what felt like a few minutes later, I heard Derrick pack up his bag and the door being locked.

I stayed under the blankets and rolled over, facing the door, and pulled his pillow under my head. I could still smell him on the sheets, and for some reason, that comforted me and allowed me to drift back into a sound sleep.

A loud bang woke me. I sat up in bed, looking around the room frantically. I could feel my heart beating wildly in my chest as I sat as still as I could. Clutching the covers to my chest, I tried calming myself down. As I looked around the room, I noticed that the curtains were still pulled tight. No one could see in and the door was still locked.

Another bang rang out, this time coming from the room next door. Wrapping the top blanket securely around my naked body, I tiptoed over to the door and looked through the peephole. I immediately felt my heart start to calm down when I saw that there was no one there. For a second, I thought Jonas had found me and that he had waited until he knew I was alone to bang on the door.

I double checked the lock and padded across the floor to the bathroom. I leaned against the counter, looking at myself in the mirror. I could see the fear across my face.

"Will I ever stop being afraid," I wondered aloud and let out the breath I was holding.

Since I couldn't answer my own question, I decided not to dwell on it and started the shower. When the water was warm, I dropped the blanket to the floor and climbed in, letting the hot water wash over my body. After twenty minutes, my skin now good and red, I climbed out and wrapped myself in one of the thin white hotel towels, the rough fabric scratching against my skin. How I missed my plush towels from back home.

I swiped at the steam covered mirror, removing the condensation, and once again studied my reflection. My stomach hurt, and the longer Derrick was gone, the more worry built within me. The longer he was gone, the more I thought about what had transpired between the two of us last night, and the more I feared it might have been a huge mistake.

It had been a stupid move on my part to sleep with him. I mean, no guy wants someone who is broken. No guy wants someone that they have to protect. We had gone way too far last night. I needed him to protect me, and I feared that things would never be the same between us again.

I went to grab my moisturizer from my bag when I heard a large bang come from the other side of the bathroom door. I jumped, causing my toiletry bag to fall to the floor, its contents scattering everywhere. Another loud thud just on the other side of the wall told me that someone was definitely in our room. I pressed my ear up to the closed bathroom door, barely breathing and straining to listen.

"Katy, it's just me," I heard Derrick's thick, deep voice call out.

Almost instantly, I felt a sense of relief wash over me, and I opened the door and stepped out in nothing but that small ratty towel. I didn't care. I just needed to know it was really him.

He stood with his back to me, his shirt tight in all the right places, showcasing every muscle he had worked on today.

"Good morning."

He turned towards me, and as soon as he set his eyes on me, they washed over me, the corner of his mouth lifting in a pleasant surprise at the way I greeted him.

"Morning."

"How was your workout?" I asked, grabbing my jeans and shirt from my bag. I couldn't help but glance over at his heavily-muscled arms and felt a sharp throb at my centre. I had always been an arm and hand girl, and Derrick had amazing arms and hands.

"It was good. Why don't you get dressed. Let's go grab

breakfast. I'm starving," he said, coming up behind me and wrapping his arm around my waist, taking the time to slowly kiss the side of my neck.

I closed my eyes, my body all warm and tingly at the feel of his lips, and I let out a throaty moan.

"All right, make any more of those noises, and I'll have you for breakfast instead." He laughed, letting me go and gently tapping my ass. "Get dressed."

Twenty minutes later, we were seated in my new car, Derrick behind the wheel and me in the passenger seat, and we drove over to a little diner that sat on the corner, promising the best all-day breakfast in the area. Here I thought that things might be awkward between us, but he behaved just like he had before last night, like this was natural, like everything between us was as normal as breathing. Maybe it was, but since I knew absolutely nothing about normal relationships, I couldn't tell. I couldn't remember the last time I had had one. I couldn't even say I'd had one as a young adult. I'd dated throughout college, if you could call it dating, but it was more overnights with very drunk frat boys. Thinking back, I couldn't even remember a single time that I had left the college campus with one of them. I didn't count those nights, though. The ones that counted were afterward, after college, when all I had attracted were guys like Jonas.

The diner was busy. We were lucky to have grabbed a table in the back of the restaurant. I was quiet as we sat across from one another, Derrick digging into his egg omelet, and me into my waffles. For once, everything inside of me was calm and natural. Derrick told me all about his upcoming fight next week, things he had been working on to improve in the ring, and why it was so important for him to win them all. He had dreams and things he wanted to accomplish—just another thing that separated him from Jonas and the other guys I had been with. I shared with him a couple of stories from the ER the other night, and he listened intently, never missing a beat, never interrupting, just listening. Somehow, the guy I had so desperately wanted to hate understood me and found small ways to treat me like I was special.

When the waitress came by our table to refill our coffee she also dropped off the bill. I went to reach for the little black billfold after the waitress had walked away, but Derrick grabbed it first saying something about him wanting things to be fair.

I frowned. "What do you mean fair?" I asked, trying to rip it from his hand.

"Never you mind, just let me pay for breakfast. Is it not okay that I want to treat you?" he said, making a funny face at me.

I didn't feel right about letting him pay when I owed him a month's payments, but I let out a laugh, and he took the bill and went up to the counter to pay, while I sat and sipped on my fresh coffee.

"Where are we going?" I questioned when Derrick

pulled out of the diner's parking lot and drove in the opposite direction of our place.

"I just wanted to stop and grab a few things that we might need," he said, pulling into the parking lot of the local Walmart.

"Here, let me give you some cash," I said, reaching for my wallet while Derrick found a parking spot.

"Katy, no, it's all right. Just wait in the car. I will be out in two minutes." He leaned over and kissed me on the cheek and hopped out of the car.

I watched him make his way across the parking lot, and once he had disappeared inside, I sat back in the seat with Derrick's baseball cap pulled down over my head and the hood from my sweater pulled up over that with my sunglasses on.

Even though Derrick didn't make me wait long, I still felt paranoid. He wasn't gone long, ten minutes perhaps, when I spotted him coming out the front door carrying a large bag, which he threw into the back seat.

"What is all that?" I asked as he started the car.

"You'll see." He winked and buckled his belt.

We drove back to the hotel, small talk going on between us. He scoped out the parking lot before letting me get out of the van. He always said I couldn't be too careful. As soon as we were back inside our room, he turned and handed the bag to me. I looked up at him, unsure what he was doing.

"Open it." He gestured.

I eyed him and then opened the bag. I pulled out two large fluffy, soft purple towels. "What are these for?" I asked, running my hands over them again and again, loving the feel of them against my skin. They sure beat the crap the hotel had.

"They are for you. I noticed how small and rough the hotel's towels were. As much as I like how they look on you, they are too rough for your soft skin. So I got you these." He smiled and placed a kiss on the top of my head.

In that moment, I just wanted to cry. He'd thought of me, thought I deserved better, and as I stood there looking down at the plush towels that lay in my hand, in my favorite color, I truly believed that I didn't deserve him.

Two weeks later, he proved that again when he found us a new place to live. It was a little more upscale than the last. He protected me and made me feel safe every single chance he got. Over time, Derrick was also the one who had initiated the changes that I was still afraid to make: settling into a new life with someone I could finally trust.

We moved into the new place on my first day off. We had just finished unpacking and I had just put dinner on to cook. This place had almost a full-sized kitchen with a stove, which made things much easier. I had just put a chicken and potatoes into the oven and finished putting broccoli into the pot on the stove. Derrick lay reading an article in one of his body building magazines, and I flopped down in the chair across from him and let out a sigh. I had many things weighing on my mind and needed to talk to him about it. I needed to bring up the uncomfortable subject of just how much I was going to owe him for his services because, after all, I had made that agreement with him and didn't want him to think I had forgotten.

"Derrick, can we talk for minute?" I asked, fidgeting with a button on my shirt.

"Sure, what's up?"

"Well, it's just today was payday for me and I...I just wanted to know how much you wanted...for, well...this."

He dropped the magazine down on his lap and looked over at me, his eyes meeting mine. I was afraid that I would insult him by still wanting to pay him after everything that had been going on between us. However, at the same time, I didn't want him to think that I had slept with him to get out of paying him either. He didn't say anything. He just looked around the room, almost as if he didn't know what to say. After almost as much silence as I could take, he cleared his throat. "How about we just go halfsies on the new place."

"That is a kind offer, but, Derrick, it doesn't seem fair to me. I mean some nights you don't sleep at all because you are too busy watching out the windows, especially when things get loud outside." I twirled my thumbs around each other. What I was asking of him was more than I could afford to pay. "How about I just pay for it all," I simply stated. I could afford it. I made good money and I would be paying it anyways without him. "That way you stay for free and put your money into your training." I smiled. I could tell instantly that he didn't like the idea, but he didn't argue with me either.

We had been living in the new place a week already and things between us had settled into a calm, comfortable existence. I was starting to feel like we had a real relationship. We respected one another, each giving one another our own space, and we never fought. Life had been quiet and wonderful in a way I never knew it could be, and there had been no more signs of Jonas being around.

On the nights I worked, Derrick would drop me off outside the employee entrance at the back and he would wait for me to get inside. He would then leave and head to the gym for his second workout of the day. He was working so hard to achieve his dream. Most nights he would text me on his way back from the gym and meet me for my break. I would bring out two hot coffees and food from the cafeteria and we would sit and talk for an hour. It allowed me to unwind from whatever was going on during my shift. Afterwards, he would go back to our place and wait until he had to come and pick me up in the morning.

On my nights off, I would accompany him to his fights. I was always afraid of him getting hurt, but he told me as long as I cheered loud enough for him to hear, he would always come out on top. So that was what I did.

CHAPTER 17

Katy

It was Monday night, the week of the big fight. It was eleven and I had just gotten off my shift and was about to start my four days off. As usual, Derrick was waiting for me when I stepped out the back door of the hospital. As soon as he spotted me, he pulled up beside the door and I climbed into the car. I was so thankful to be able to sit down and relax; my body was tired. We drove back to our place, him listening patiently as I told him about my night. I was venting about that plastic surgeon again, who had once again asked me out on a date.

"Do I need to pay him a visit?" he asked, chuckling to himself.

"No, Derrick, it's fine."

"You sure? Because, honestly, one visit—a good busted-up face again—and he will be back to picking on me and leave you alone." He grabbed hold of my knee and tickled me. I grabbed his hand and tried to pull it away, but I was laughing too hard as he continued to tickle me. Even though I knew Derrick was serious about it, I never feared that he would come unglued and come after the guy.

I looked over at Derrick, once he had let my knee go, the serious look on his face returning. He got quiet as he continued driving towards our place. "Is everything okay?" All of a sudden, I was worried about Derrick. He never let his guard down even for a second when it came to me, even when I complained about someone as non-threatening as Dr. Good Looking. He looked exhausted. The double workouts, side fights at night, and barely any sleep, I didn't know how he stayed on alert all the time.

"Of course. Just tired," he said, interlocking his fingers with mine and concentrating back on the road.

When we walked through the door of the apartment, I headed straight for the shower, while Derrick secured our room for the night. It was a new place, and I was back to not being able to sleep unless the dresser was pulled in front of the door, and every night, Derrick made sure to move it there.

Twenty minutes later, I emerged from the bathroom wearing my racer-back and boy shorts. Derrick already had all the lights off and was lying in bed, in his usual boxers, flipping through the channels.

"I figured you would be asleep already," I mumbled, crawling in beside him.

"Nah, thought I would wait for you," he answered and let out a yawn, holding his arms open for me to crawl into.

I curled up beside him, resting my head on his chest, and let my tired body relax against his warmth. He shut the TV off and wrapped his arm around me, pulling me tighter against him, and I closed my eyes, relaxing in the safety of his arms. This was our normal. Sometimes...there was sex, other times not, either way, he never complained and never shoved me away; we would just fall into a deep sleep together. He normally didn't sleep much during the night. He would just basically nap on and off until it was time for him to get up and go to the gym. In the mornings, especially my days off, he would be careful not to wake me while getting ready, but I normally stirred when he would remove his body from mine. The warmth and security he provided me had become my blanket, one I didn't care to leave.

I felt his hand squeeze my hip, and I rolled over and murmured his name. "It's okay, babe. You stay. Stay in...just stay in bed until I get back. It's too early for you to get up." He placed a lingering kiss on my bare shoulder, just like he did every morning.

"Do you have to go?" I murmured.

"You know I do," he said, falling back into bed and kissing my neck.

"I'll get up, come with you," I said, struggling to pull from his grip.

"No, sweetie, get some rest. I will be back soon." He gently kissed my neck again, whispering into my ear how he couldn't wait to get back to me. That was all I needed to hear, his words, his touch, his kiss sending me back into a deep sleep.

I woke when I heard the shower running. Normally, I would already be up by the time he was back, but not this morning. I rubbed at my tired eyes and lay there in time to catch a glimpse of Derrick, naked, in the mirror in the bathroom through the crack of the door. He always showered with the door open a crack, in case I needed him for something. A simple glance at his ass as he climbed into the shower proved to be dangerous to me, and I felt my body stir.

I stretched and got up from the warmth of our bed, dropping what little I wore in a pile on the floor. Calm and confident, I strode across the room to the bathroom and quietly pushed the curtain aside and climbed into the shower with him. He didn't have a chance to turn around before I was already running my hands down his strong back and kissing his shoulder. He slowly turned towards me and pulled me under the hot water. He didn't wait. He grabbed me under my ass, while I wrapped my arms around his neck, and lifting me, he placed me against the wall of the shower.

He attacked my mouth, running his strong hand

through my hair, while the other rested under my ass. "Wrap your legs around my waist." He moaned into my mouth, as he sucked my bottom lip. I did as he instructed, wrapping my legs around his waist, hooking my feet together. His tongue swept through my mouth as his hands gripped my ass tightly.

My centre was throbbing by the time the water started to run cold. I needed him inside of me. He shut the water off and carried me to the bed and lay me down. "Get onto your knees."

"What?" I asked, reaching for his hands, but he tore them from me.

"On your knees."

I looked up at him, a little afraid at first. Jonas used to be demanding like this, and he used to love to fuck this way, fucking me so hard I would eventually cry out in pain. Derrick wouldn't have known that, and I swallowed hard, afraid to say anything, finally doing as he asked and rolling onto my knees. I looked back over my shoulder at Derrick, who was already checking out my backside, a gleam in his eye I hadn't seen before. He ran his hands lightly over my ass, which sent chills through me. He was touching me the exact way that Jonas used to before he punished me. I closed my eyes and swallowed hard as I felt his strong hands rest on my hips and he pulled me back a little bit.

"You're the perfect woman," Derrick moaned as he slid slowly inside of me, filling me, causing me to moan out loud. He pumped into me so slow and deep; it was almost like torture. There was no nasty talk, no hard thrusting, no hitting, just love making and soft caresses. I could already feel him swelling inside of me with each torturous stroke. He wrapped his arm around my waist and pulled me up so my back was against his chest, and he turned my head with his free hand, meeting my lips. His other hand slid down between my legs and he began stroking my clit in quick, short strokes as his cock hit the perfect spot inside of me. "Come for me, baby. I want to feel you tighten around my cock," he whispered, kissing my ear.

He was relentless, pumping into me still painfully slow and deep, and I could feel myself tighten with every stroke of his fingers. Every touch was like lightning coursing through my body.

"Fuck me, you're so fucking tight," he whimpered, his voice shaking. He pumped into me a couple more times, and we both let go, coming together.

It was the most intense orgasm I had ever experienced as he collapsed on top of me, his arms catching him. I could still feel him throbbing inside of me as he rested for a second, trying to catch his breath. "My God that was amazing," he whispered, kissing my shoulder.

He pulled himself from me and I laid down on the bed, grabbing the messy covers and pulling them around me. He, too, collapsed into the bed and looked into my eyes. His large hand came up to rest on my cheek. "I meant what I said, Katy," he whispered. "You are the perfect woman."

I hid my eyes from him. To me he was the perfect man, which made being the perfect woman very easy. I wasn't used to the compliments, and it made me uneasy that he was saying these things to me. His hand still resting on my cheek, he leaned in and kissed me.

CHAPTER 18

Dagger

It was Friday, I had just returned from the gym, excited to see Katy before she left for work. I walked into our place and dropped my bag on the floor. I could hear the shower running, and I called out to Katy to let her know it was me and went straight to our little kitchen area to make my shake.

I had just finished shoving veggies into the cup when Katy came out of the bathroom, her hair wrapped in the purple towel I bought her and the other one wrapped around her body. She gave me a sexy smile and grabbed her hairbrush.

"You are sure there is no way for you not to work tonight?" I asked her as I shoved a few berries into my blender cup. I hated to ask, but I was finding it tough to be both the bodyguard and the MMA fighter while she was at work.

Normally, I was off at night while she worked. It made it easy, and she didn't have a clue, but those nights, I would spend all evening out in the hospital parking lot just in case she needed me. I would drop her off, make sure she had gotten into the building, and then I would park and sit in the car until she sent me a text letting me know she was clocking out and I could pick her up at the door.

I don't know why, but for some reason, she never questioned how I had managed to get there so quickly. Maybe she thought I was simply showing up early and that it all just came together. Whatever it was, it really didn't matter.

Tonight, though, it did matter. Tonight was the night of the big fight. Truthfully, it wasn't just because I would worry about her while she was at work. I wanted her there, cheering me on. Tonight the scouts would be out looking.

She looked over at me. "Why do you want me to call in?" she asked, running the brush through her wet hair.

"It's just, well, tonight I'm going to be later," I warned. "This is a big fight. I'm the last bout of the night—the main event. There are going to be agents there looking to possibly sign me, and if that happens, things will be even later. I guess I would feel better if you were there, where I knew you were safe. Plus, you could cheer me on."

She shook her head and continued packing up her own bag for work. "I wish I could, but you know I hate seeing you get hurt, but I do want to be there to support you. It's just, I can't get the night off. One of the other nurses has a sick kid. Plus, the flu is going around, and we have been more slammed than normal." She sighed as she threw her scrubs into her bag. "It will be just like any other night: I'll be busy and I'll be safe. I'll wait for you to call to tell me you are leaving the fight. Maybe you'll even come in to get stitched up. It'll almost be like a date." She winked at me, giggling.

"Ha-ha, very funny." I drank down my shake and threw a change of clothes into my bag. "No, there is a difference. Any other night, I'd be out in the parking lot your entire shift," I mumbled as I continued throwing in more items.

"What did you just say?" The quiver in her voice made me turn and look at her. Her face had lost the pretty pink color that she normally had. She stood there frozen, blinking a few times.

I took a deep breath. I didn't think she would have heard me. I walked over and placed my hands on her shoulders. "I watch out for you. I stay out in the parking lot. I've never just dropped you off and left."

She swallowed hard. I wasn't sure if I was in deep shit and should duck or not after all she had been through. "You spend ten to twelve hours in a parking lot...waiting for me?"

I chuckled. "Well, not exactly...I mean...I come in to pee and get something to eat. You know they really should leave that little cafe open in the lobby longer than they do. They have good stuff in there."

She surprised me by wrapping her arms around my midsection and resting her head against my chest. In turn, I wrapped my arms around her and kissed the top of her head. "Tonight you are going to have to drive yourself. I am not all that comfortable with any of this," I said, shaking my head.

"I'll be fine, I promise. I'll wait for you and you can follow me home. Now let me get a good look at you while you can still open both of your eyes."

She looked up into my face, smiling. Home. I loved the sound of that—a place that we shared together. "I've never lived with a woman before," I whispered as I brushed a few stray hairs from her face and kissed her forehead.

"Really? You sure about that? I mean you keep the toilet seat down. I was sure you were a pro."

I wrapped my arms around her tighter. "Nah, I just try to be considerate, make you happy," I said, pressing my lips to hers.

"It's working. I've never felt like this before."

I kept watching her, the look in her eye growing serous as she stared back at me.

"Is it too soon for me to be thinking that I love you?"

My breath caught in my throat as the words left her lips. I knew how I felt about her, but I didn't think she felt the same. "Well..." I cleared my throat. "This could be a product of the situation. You know, like, you're not used to a guy like me." I shrugged, trying to play it off.

"I guess you might be right." She sighed and placed her forehead down on my chest. I ran my fingers into her soft, silky hair and let my fingers massage her scalp.

"Well, maybe I am right, but that wouldn't explain why I love you too." My face flamed as the words fell from my lips. Another first for me: I had never told a woman that. At least, not one I wasn't related to. I pulled her closer to me and held her. "Nothing can happen to you. Got it? Stay at the hospital. I will come for you."

"Okay. I promise. Please don't worry. I will wait for you." She ran her hand down my arm and laced her fingers with mine, then reached up to meet my lips. "All right, let's get you packed up for tonight, shall we?" she said as she kissed me one more time, taking her lips from mine.

CHAPTER 19

Katy

I SHUT my locker and hummed to myself as I made my way to the nurses' desk in the ER. A slight smile played on my lips at the thought of the intimate moment that Derrick and I had shared before we both left tonight.

I nodded at one of the doctors as I grabbed a cup of coffee and continued quietly humming the melody of one of my favorite songs as I made my way to my station. Mollie was already seated behind her computer and gave me a funny look as I took a seat beside her. "Wow."

"What?" I asked as I sat down behind my computer and logged in.

"Looks like someone is love!" Mollie teased. I could

feel the blush rising to my cheeks as she tilted her head. "Anyone I know?"

I knew she had been watching that plastic surgeon chase after me since I had started here, and I wanted to dispel that myth immediately. I didn't need any office gossip going around about me. I also knew that she had been watching me go on my break to go to the cafeteria to meet Derrick every night for weeks. That was abnormal behavior for me. Normally, I just munched on popcorn behind my computer and worked on my paperwork during my break. I typed in my password and shrugged. "His name is Derrick."

Mollie's forehead furrowed. "Derrick? Which doctor is that? Do I know Derrick?"

I snickered at her confusion. I knew she hadn't been expecting that answer. "He isn't a doctor. I think you called him Dagger." I giggled as her eyes widened in shock.

"I'm so happy for you! He's one of the good ones. Plus, he is nice on the eyes as well." She laughed, placing her hand on my shoulder. "Good for you, Katy. You deserve happiness. So does he. You want anything from the vending machine?" she asked, getting up and wrapping her sweater around her.

"No, I'm good, thanks. Already got my coffee," I said, nodding to my cup.

"Okay, I will be right back."

For some reason, even though I had told myself it didn't matter what anyone thought, I was glad she liked him, and that someone finally approved of a relationship I was in. Even if that someone really had no bearing on my life whatsoever. I had never gotten any kind of reassurance from anyone when it had come to Jonas, or any other previous boyfriend, for that matter. Her approval actually made me feel hopeful; hopeful that I had for once had chosen a good guy.

I began reading the notes about all the patients on the floor currently when I felt someone staring at me. I looked up and there stood the pretty boy plastic surgeon on the other side of my desk looking down at me, smiling.

"Can I help you?" I did my best not to show the annoyance on my face. He had no reason whatsoever to be up here.

"Katy, sweet Katy, when are you going to take me up on my offer? I happen to have a room booked at the Marriott this weekend in the city and dinner for two at that new expensive steakhouse. What do you say?"

"I say I don't think my boyfriend, Derrick, will approve. You remember him don't you, doc? He was in here a little while ago for some stitches above the eye. Big guy, fighter. Surely, you remember," I said, taking a sip of my coffee.

Mollie slid in beside me and looked from Dr. Pretty Boy to me. "Hey, doc! What are you doing all the way up here? We didn't call you," she said from her seat.

"Oh geez, I've got to go," he said, fiddling with his

pager, the look on his face telling me I didn't have to worry about him anymore.

"Have a good night, doc. We will call if we need you."

As soon as he was gone, I turned to Mollie. "He came up here to ask me on a date. I let him know I wasn't interested."

Mollie let out a laugh and shook her head. I didn't have a chance to take another sip of my coffee because an ambulance showed up and the chaos began. Two victims due to a car crash. Typical start to a weekend: people partying too hard at the beach who decide they are more than fine to get in a car and drive. Before long, I was so wrapped up in doing my job that I barely had time to watch the time pass. As soon as we had stabilized the first set of patients, in came two other ambulances, two more car accident victims, followed by one gunshot victim and a stabbing. By the time I got a second to finally glance up, it was nearly eleven. I knew Derrick would be fighting soon, and I wanted to send him words of encouragement since I couldn't be there.

I removed my dirty gloves, washed my hands, and started walking towards the nurses' station when the doctor on call handed me a couple of files.

"Katy, could you please update the computers and get those labs sent down ASAP."

"Sure thing." I nodded and took the files from him and made my way to my desk. I had almost perfect timing. No one was around, so I took two seconds and grabbed my cell phone from my purse and quickly sent Derrick a message.

ME: LOVE YOU, DERRICK. GO KICK BUTT. AND PUNCH FACE. AND DO WHATEVER ELSE IT TAKES NOT TO END UP IN THE EMERGENCY ROOM FOR ANY OTHER REASON THAN TO MEET ME. IT'S BUSY IN HERE TONIGHT.

I HIT send and sat down behind my computer and quickly entered the patients' information into their respective charts. Then I called for lab pickup. I glanced at my phone before going back. I didn't expect to hear from Derrick, but there was a message waiting for me.

DERRICK: I LOVE YOU TOO. SEE YOU SOON! I GOTTA GO WIN THIS FIGHT.

HE ENDED the message with a winky face kissing emoji, which filled my heart. I felt confident that he would do well, and I returned my phone to my purse and headed back in the direction of the next patient.

It was midnight by the time I had returned from my first quick break of the night. I had decided to stay and help out with what I could until Derrick called to tell me he was on his way. We were still slammed, so they were grateful for the extra set of hands.

I quickly shoved the last piece of banana into my mouth when one of the girls from the registration area came over to Mollie and me. "Hey, ladies, there's a guy out front. Says that someone hit a black SUV." She rattled off the license plate. "Does it belong to any of you? Police are out front taking a report. Apparently a hit and run."

I swallowed hard. My new car. "That is my plate." I frowned. I was parked in the employee lot, but due to some construction that was being done, that lot wasn't as secure as it normally was. Lately, non-employees could and did sneak in and park there, since you didn't have to pay, but it was unusual for there to be an accident.

"Well, you better go out there and talk to them and see what's up," she added and turned to head back to her station.

I stood looking after the girl from registration. Mollie glanced at me before she murmured, "You better see what's up."

I shrugged. "I'll be right back." I shoved my cell phone into the pocket of my top and rushed out the back of the emergency department and straight across the lot to where my vehicle was parked in the employee lot. When I got out there I realized that I had made a horrific mistake.

There were no flashing lights, there were no police, and there was also no Derrick watching for me throughout my shift.

My stomach started to turn, and I decided to turn on my heels before I ever even made it all the way to my vehicle. That was when Jonas stepped out of the shadows behind me, blocking my path back to the hospital.

A sense of dread coursed through me as I realized he had been watching and waiting and I had fallen victim to the perfect trap. Jonas had found me and he stood a few feet across from me, staring. I slowly began to back away. I knew I wasn't going to be able to outrun him; I never could. I had my keys in my hand, and I glanced around the parking lot to see if anyone was out there, but there wasn't a single, solitary person who could help me. Shift change had already happened, so unless someone was leaving work early, I was all alone until security did their rounds at four. I should have known Jonas would do his research. He had probably been watching this place for months, which meant he would know about Derrick.

I suddenly wished that I had listened to Derrick. He had begged me that under no circumstances was I to leave that hospital. Why hadn't I been smart and told the girl from registration to have the police meet me in the emergency area? I glanced around the area praying that perhaps one of the guards was out for a smoke break tonight.

"If you're looking for your security guards, there's a

fight on the other side of the hospital. I reported it. They all ran off like little puppets to save some helpless victim." He grinned, his voice sending waves of unease throughout my body. He was smarter than I gave him credit for. "Well, there isn't really a fight, of course, but it gives me time."

I swallowed hard as I continued to back up slowly. "Time...time for what?"

"Time to teach you a lesson and remind you who the boss is." His eyes darkened as he lunged at me. I turned and started to race away, running in and around the cars. I was smaller and more nimble than Jonas. He was big, bulky, but he had strength on his side. I ran hard and tried to circle around and make it back to the door, but I didn't win. He grabbed my scrub shirt and yanked me backwards, sending me down to the pavement, my head connecting with the cement. My eyes rolled back into my head and I struggled hard to open them up in time to see him standing over me. He delivered one solid, hard punch to my face. I felt the explosion of pain across my cheekbone, and this time, when my head connected again with the pavement, everything went dark.

CHAPTER 20

Dagger

THE BELL RANG OUT, letting me know I had won the first round with a knockout. Coach called me over to the side and squirted water into my mouth. "You were quick on your feet. You did awesome. Last round, get 'em, Dag."

I didn't know how I had done it. The whole time I had been thinking about Katy and what she had said. The only reason she wanted to see me in the ER tonight was to pick her up; she didn't want me coming in there all beaten and broken. She had no idea how opposed to that idea I was as well. This match was huge, and there were agents everywhere, scouting and looking for their next star, and their next star would definitely not be the one who ended up in the emergency room.

"Word has it two of the scouts from Vegas are here. You've got to do this, Dag. Keep going and fucking win!"

I was pumped as the starting bell for the next round sounded. Adrenaline coursed through my veins, and every hit, punch, and kick I made was for my girl. No sooner had my opponent hit the floor, the bell sounded and I was proclaimed the winner. I climbed out of the ring, and within seconds, coach and I were surrounded by several agents. Some I recognized, others I didn't, but each one represented different groups in the MMA industry. As I was pulled and questioned, I wished from the bottom of my heart that Katy could be here; she would be so proud. I was eager to share this with her.

I spoke to each agent as I made my way down the line. They all had one thing in common: each one of them was based out west. One was from LA, another from Seattle, a couple more from LA, and the final one from Vegas. The bright lights of the Vegas MMA were finally calling to me, and I couldn't wait to talk to my girl.

"Before I commit to anything, I will need to speak to my girl and decide where she wants to relocate to," I told each one of the agents, not shooting any of them down right away. I wanted Katy's input on this decision. "She's a nurse, and she is working right now." I chuckled. "I'm just lucky that I don't need her services right now. Can I let you know on Monday what we decide?"

Each of them nodded, were completely understanding, and they all shoved a card into my hand and begged me to call. I pushed through the crowd to the changing room. I was eager to get cleaned up and go see her at the hospital. I showered and dressed, received my payout, and made my way to my car. I was walking on air. At almost close to nine grand, this was the biggest payout I had ever won and would easily cover us for three months of living and gym expenses. I grinned and pulled out my phone. I couldn't wait to get there to tell her; I needed to let her know now. I needed to hear her voice.

I threw my bag into the back of my car and got into the driver's seat, first pulling my phone from my pocket. I pulled my belt across me and stared down at the screen of my phone. There were a slew of missed calls, messages, and one single text from an unknown number. My gut churned and my heart sank. Something was wrong. I read the text first to see if it told me anything before I dove into the messages. It was Mollie from the hospital.

MOLLIE: I GOT YOUR NUMBER FROM YOUR MEDICAL FILE, PLEASE DO NOT REPORT ME, ITS AN EMERGENCY, KATY IS MISSING

I QUICKLY SEARCHED my contacts and pulled up the hospital information. I was put through to Mollie within minutes of stating who I was.

"Mollie, it's Derrick, what is going on?" I asked, trying to remain calm, even though every part of me was vibrating. I had let my girl down.

"Hey, Derrick, they told us that her vehicle had been hit and she needed to meet the police outside. She never came back. Security checked her car. It's fine, not a mark on it. It's still in the parking lot, but she is gone. They are reviewing the security cameras right now."

"Well, where the fuck did she go?" I demanded into the phone.

"That's not all. They found blood droplets in the parking lot and a dent in a hood of another car. Do you know anything?"

I let out a breath. Thank God; it didn't sound like they were suspecting me. At least, I didn't think so. "Listen, Mollie, I am going to send you a picture. Please give it to the police. Katy was running from an ex-boyfriend. He may have something to do with this. Actually, I am almost positive it's him. I am on my way. I will attach the details."

I hung up and searched my phone for that picture of Jonas I had taken. I attached it to a message for Mollie.

ME: SHE WAS RUNNING FROM AN ABUSIVE EX. HIS NAME IS JONAS, NO IDEA OF HIS LAST NAME. I WAS SUPPOSED TO BE PROTECTING HER.

WITHOUT WAITING FOR A REPLY, I dropped my phone down in the console and reversed out of the spot. I was overcome with guilt. I had totally let her down and didn't do my job. I didn't blame her at all for this. I should have turned down this fight when she wouldn't come with me. After all, there would be more. There wouldn't be more Katy if he got his hands on her. If I had been in the parking lot, this wouldn't have happened, and she would be safe with me, wrapped in my arms in bed by now, not out there alone with him.

At the next light, I skidded to a stop after remembering I had her on the Find My Friend app. I opened my phone and quickly messaged Mollie.

ME: I HAVE HER ON FIND MY FRIEND. I'M GOING TO CHECK IT RIGHT NOW. IF HER PHONE IS ON AND WITH HER, WE WILL KNOW. ARE POLICE THERE TO RELAY INFORMATION TO?

MOLLI: YES, GREAT IDEA

Her response was quick and short, which meant she was waiting for me to get her more information. I pulled up the app and blinked hard at what I was seeing. That couldn't be right. The location had her marked at being at our apartment, and I knew she had left with her phone because we had messaged shortly before I had gotten into the ring. I quickly texted the address over to Mollie and asked her to tell the officer I was on my way.

My phone let out a shrill ring, and as soon as I picked it up, I heard Mollie on the other end. "Derrick, he says to wait. The officers want you to wait for them to arrive," she pleaded into the phone.

I hung up without answering. I wasn't waiting. This was Katy, my girl, and I wasn't going to let her face Jonas alone.

I flew through red lights and rushed to the extended-stay. There were no police there yet when I arrived. I didn't wait; I couldn't. I jumped out of the car, ran to our room, and with my keycard in hand, I slid it into the slot and was about to touch the handle to open the door when I heard Katy shout, "No!"

I paused, unsure what I should do. Then I heard a sound I would know anywhere: the sound of her being hit, the connecting of skin and her cries of pain. I opened the door with a kick, quickly dropping beside the build-ing. Who the hell knew if the psycho had a gun or some-thing else. I glanced around the corner and quickly realized that he had rigged the handle. He had a battery in there with jumper cables. I could've been killed had I touched the handle, but thanks to Katy's warning, I wasn't.

I scrambled to my feet. The guy wasn't a fair fighter. I gathered that from the target he had chosen. Katy was too kind, too nice, and probably too quick to give him any more chances. I'd never need more than one chance with her, because I certainly wasn't going to blow it.

She was seated in a chair at the farthest point across the room. He stood behind her, his hands around her throat. "Come any closer and I will make sure she doesn't take another breath," he sneered.

"Get away from her," I growled.

"Why should I?" He began tightening his hands around her throat. She began to claw and grasp at hands while trying to gasp for breath. In a matter of seconds, she was already turning color. "If I can't have her...no one will."

I wasn't sure if he could choke her out before I got to her, or if he planned to snap her neck in one quick motion if I got too close. Either way, I wasn't going to allow it. I glared the guy down, adrenaline racing through me. I prayed the police showed up soon because when I got my hands on him, I had no idea what I would be capable of.

I could see his knuckles whitening now, and Katy was blue, her eyes starting to bulge and go red. There wasn't going to be much time; I couldn't wait. I immediately launched myself toward the guy. He was startled enough that he released her, and to ensure her safety, I pushed her chair out of the way with my body, knocking her roughly to the side.

"Sorry..." I yelled as Jonas came at me. I grabbed him and began grappling with the guy. He was a dirty fighter and his shots were cheap but not unlike some of the fighters I faced in the ring. I planned to get him subdued and restrained before the police arrived, but I was too late. Before I could get my arms around him, two officers charged into the room. I was too involved in dealing with Jonas but was sure Katy would tell them I was the good guy. I was finally on top of him and winning when an officer came at me. I was grateful for the extra hand, but instead, he raised his taser before I could say anything. He touched the taser to my back, and I stiffened, rolling off Jonas and onto the floor. Jonas jumped up and attacked the officer who had tased me in an effort to get back to Katy; however, the second officer tased him before he got any farther. Within seconds, they cuffed him, picked him up, and carried him downstairs. Seconds later, I too felt the cold metal connecting with the skin around my wrists.

"No, not him. He was trying to save me," I heard Katy's breathless, scratchy voice call out.

My head dropped to the floor. He had finally been caught, and I could hear my girl's voice. She was okay. The cuffs came off, and as I lay there trying to catch my breath, I tried to get over my anger at the police. I rolled onto my back and felt the sting of the spot where the probes were still attached to me from the taser. More than likely I would have to go to the hospital to have them removed.

I sat up. I wanted to make sure Katy was safe, and I watched as the officers helped her. As soon as she was able to, she rushed into my arms, straddling my lap, crying. I held her tight to me, trying to warm her cold body. She had gone into a little bit of shock after the ordeal with Jonas and was freezing. "Are you okay?" she murmured into my neck.

My girl had been taken from me and tied to a chair, almost choked out, and here she was asking me if I was okay. "I'm fine, Katy, barely a scratch," I said, running my hand through her hair and down her cheek, cupping it. I kissed her softly, and soon we were being escorted out of the room. Minutes later, we were both seated in the back of an ambulance being checked over. I insisted they check over Katy numerous times before they even touched me, and once they had deemed her to be fine, she sat between my legs, my arms wrapped around her, while the paramedic removed the taser probes from my back.

Now alone in the ambulance, Katy turned her tiny body so her chest was facing mine and rested her head on my shoulder, my arms wrapped around her. We stayed that way until we heard a throat clear and Katy's name called. We both looked up to see an officer standing before us.

"Katy, we would like to ask you a few questions," the officer said, pulling a notepad from his back pocket.

She looked to me, fear in her eyes. "It's okay, breathe," I urged, rubbing her back. "You got this, and I have you," I reminded her, pressing my lips to her temple.

"Even after all of this?" she whispered, her face a picture of shock and wonder.

"Especially after all this."

She sat between my legs, while the officer questioned her. Her mind was a jumble and she struggled to answer the questions that were being asked. Every once in a while I would feel her body stiffen, and I would gently rub her arm and rest my hand on her waist, letting her know I was still there and that it was okay for her to take her time. Her body shook as she recounted some of the things she told the officer, her voice strong, but then the tears would fall. But she was as strong as I knew she could be with me behind her.

When all the questions had been asked, we watched the cruisers drive away, Jonas looking out from the window of the back seat. Katy turned and buried her face in my neck; she didn't want to see him.

"And you, sir, we are just going to take you into the hospital. I couldn't get one of the probes out. Plus, we want a thorough check over on Katy."

Katy looked up at him. "Is he okay?" she asked, her voice hoarse as she stepped out of the way so the paramedic could strap me in. She was more concerned about me than herself.

"Yes, but that other probe needs to be removed. You

can come along for the ride if you like, or you can ride in the other ambulance."

"I'll stay here." She sat across from me, a small smirk coming to her lips.

I looked over at her and smiled. "I told you I would meet you at the hospital."

CHAPTER 21

Katy

THE POLICE FOLLOWED behind us to the hospital where
they finished taking my statement and asking any other
questions they needed answers to.

"Everything go okay?" Derrick asked as I walked
through the curtain to his room.

"Yes. They said they would call if they had any more
questions," I said, going over and standing beside him. I
hadn't wanted to leave Derrick's side while he had the
probes removed, but I had to. He wrapped his arm around
me while the nurse continued to try to remove the last
probe.

As he sat there wincing, he looked just as grumpy as

he had the night I met him, only this time I wasn't intimidated by him; I was completely head-over-heels in love with him. I let out a small laugh as he grumbled at the nurse again as she ran an alcohol swab over the area after she had finally removed the probe and quickly bandaged it.

She rolled her eyes at me. "I'll be right back. I need to get the doctor."

"Be nice," I whispered to Derrick as soon as she had left the room. "You have that look again."

"What? What look?" He looked at me, feigning innocence. "I didn't do anything."

"You, sir, are cranky," I said, pushing my way between his legs to kiss his lips.

"That's because it fucking hurts," he said, smiling against my mouth, kissing me.

"Katy! My God, there you are!" Mollie said, rushing into the room. "They told me you were on your way in. Are you all right?" she cried out, rushing over and hugging me.

"Hey, Mollie. Yeah, I'm good," I answered, putting on a brave face when all I really wanted to do was fall apart.

"Why didn't you say anything, that you were in trouble? I would have helped you," she said as she let go of me and I returned to Derrick's side, his arm slipping back around me.

I didn't really have an answer to that, except that I didn't trust many people. She was about to say something else when the doctor came rushing into the room. "Katy, we are so glad you are all right. You ready for your CT scan? They have an empty room now just for you."

I nodded. "I'm ready. I guess." Dr. Evans wanted me to have this CT scan only because I had lost consciousness when Jonas had attacked me in the parking lot and again when he had choked me.

"I can take her down, doc," Mollie said, stepping up beside me.

"I'm not an invalid. I do remember where imaging is," I said, each and every one of them laughing.

Mollie looked at me and smiled. "I think she's fine," she told Dr. Evans, who handed Mollie my chart. "Still better to be safe than sorry." She grabbed a wheelchair and patted the seat for me.

I rolled my eyes and hopped into the wheelchair just to make Mollie happy, and she started taking me from the room. "Just one minute, Mollie," I said, turning back to Derrick. "Come with me?" I asked.

He jumped up off the chair and walked beside me, holding my hand the entire way. When we finally arrived outside of the area and Mollie had left to go speak with one of the nurses and give them the paperwork, I realized that with everything that had happened tonight, I hadn't asked Derrick about his fight.

"So, how did it go tonight?" I asked quietly, squeezing his hand.

"Well, I was afraid I was going to lose you. It wasn't a

good feeling." He shook his head and kissed my cheek. I could read the worry and fear in his eyes.

I groaned. "No, crazy man, I meant the fight."

He lifted his eyes to meet mine and his face brightened. "Oh, I won that."

I squealed in delight. "Most important fight of the night and my babe wins!" I murmured, acknowledging that he was really the main event.

He shook his head. "No, that was the fight with Jonas, and we won that. He can't hurt you anymore, babe." He cupped my face. "You look terrible," he grumbled, looking at my bruises that I was sure were very dark by now. "I'm so sorry I didn't get to him before he laid his hands on you."

I shook my head slightly. My head, face, and neck hurt. "I should have listened to you. If I'd have stayed in the hospital—"

He placed his fingers up to my lips, silencing me. "He wasn't going to stop, Katy. He was going to find another way. Even if you had been with me tonight instead of here, he would have found another way." He pressed his forehead against mine while I considered his words.

"You're probably right. It's over now. What ever will we do with ourselves?"

"Well, I was going to wait to mention this to you, but since you asked..." He took a deep breath and pressed his forehead to mine again. "I have been offered a chance to sign. We have a choice of three places. Seattle, LA, or Vegas. Where would you like to go?"

"We?" I grinned.

"Well, I've already made up my mind and I have decided that I'm not going anywhere without you. So if you say you want to stay here, we will do that." He shrugged. "However, if you want to go, you should know that you're my dream girl, Katy. Fighting is my career, but I want you to be life. I realized that for the first time. I believe I could actually do other things if I have to."

I could feel tears pricking my eyes at his words. I knew his dream, and I knew what he had given up and what it took for him to make it a reality. I also knew I wasn't going to let him down. "How does Vegas sound?" I whispered.

"For real?" He brightened.

"Yes." I nodded as tears trickled down my cheeks.

"What'll we do in Vegas?" he asked with a grin.

I shrugged. "You know, the usual. Live, love, and fight." I giggled. "And we can get married by Elvis if we'd like." I let out a little laugh. I was joking, but Derrick's face grew serious, and I was suddenly afraid that I had divulged too much and had ruined the moment.

"We're ready for you, Katy." I tore my eyes from Derrick's and looked towards the tech who was waiting for me in the doorway, then looked back at Derrick.

"Don't worry, I was just joking," I mumbled, and went to walk behind the curtain.

"Serious," he responded. "We'll go to Vegas. And one day, we will get married there. It sounds like the perfect life."

I smiled, even though it hurt my now surely bruised cheek. I walked back over to Derrick and wrapped my arms around his neck. "Thank you, Dagger. Thank you for giving me my life back."

Dear Readers,

I would like to thank you for taking the time to read *Dagger*. I hope you enjoyed Derrick and Katy's story. If you did, I would love it if you would drop me a review. Reviews are so important and really help me; I love to hear what my readers think.

I would really like to thank each of you who have supported me throughout the last couple of years. This journey has been amazing so far, and I look forward to many more years of bringing you stories to get lost in.

I have many things planned for 2020. I am very excited to see what the next year is going to bring. I will be announcing each project when I am able, but for right now, Malone Brother lovers take a quick peak at what is coming to you May 29th.

Finding Forever with You
(The Malone Brothers Book 4)
Release Date: May 29, 2020

My best friend Sophie was gorgeous, at times uptight and desperate.

Her biological clock was ticking and after yet another failed relationship she pulled me aside.

"Listen Chase, you know I adore you and you know I need you. Historically, you always come through for me." She swallowed hard while I listened. "It's no secret that I want a baby, the semi old fashioned way."

I nodded not really believing what I was hearing.

"I want you to do it."

"You want my swimmers?"

"Yes, through natural injection."

Sex with my best friend. The best friend I had once upon a time wanted in a bad way.

"Don't worry, I've got this covered," I assured her. She looked relieved and maybe even a little excited.

Seven Days, Six nights, and lots of sex. What more could I want?

Oh right. A way to turn this into forever so I could raise my child too.

Preorder Today

Add to Goodreads

ABOUT THE AUTHOR

S.L. Sterling had been an avid reader since she was a child, often found getting lost in books. Today, if she isn't writing or plotting, she can be found buried in a romance novel. S.L. Sterling lives with her husband and dogs in Northern Ontario.

Sign up for my
Newsletter

Visit my
Website

Join my Street Team
Sterlings Silver Sapphires